Praise for

THEN MAY THE SENSES FALL

"I think her work is essential for anyone seeking an authentic Christian mysticism that refuses to be confined by its historical boundary of the cloister." —**Carl McColman**, author of *The New Big Book of Christian Mysticism*

"This volume makes a significant contribution to the study of Evelyn Underhill's work by gathering in one volume these selections from her early fiction and poetry, including one published here for the first time. With fresh insights into her early mystical sensibility, the short stories collected here also provide an immersive read!" —**Kathleen Henderson Staudt**, president, Evelyn Underhill Association

"Underhill's fiction invites us to enter the provocative landscape of the spirit. This book juxtaposes poetry, fiction, and commentary in a way that thrills the reader, providing a new perspective on, and way to experience, Underhill's more well-known writing on mysticism." —**Jessica L. Malay**, emeritus professor of English, University of Huddersfield; author of E*velyn Underhill and the Christian Social Movement*

"With this illuminating collection of Evelyn Underhill's early short fiction and poetry, Bill Gillard and Robert Stauffer shine a light on a key period in the development of one of mysticism's foremost advocates. Combined with Underhill's revealing essay 'A Defence of Magic,' these works channel some of her first eclectic explorations along the border between mundane and spiritual experience. Gillard's and Stauffer's perceptive and accessible commentaries offer readers insightful guidance while helpfully situating Underhill in the esoteric milieu of her time." **—James H. Thrall**, Knight Distinguished Chair Emeritus for the Study of Religion and Culture at Knox College; author of *Mystic Moderns: Agency and Enchantment in Evelyn Underhill, May Sinclair, and Mary Webb*

"Evelyn Underhill was a captivating storyteller. Her short stories are thought-provoking and filled with mystery. It is wonderful to have them all in one place and interspersed with some of her poetry plus short reflections." **—Robyn Wrigley-Carr**, author of *The Spiritual Formation of Evelyn Underhill*

"Through her short stories and poems, Underhill reminds us that sometimes art is the best philosophy." **—Diego Pérez Lasserre, PhD**, author of "Mysticism and Practical Rationality: Exploring Evelyn Underhill through the Lens of Phronesis"

THEN MAY THE SENSES FALL

EVELYN UNDERHILL'S *FORGOTTEN FICTION*

EDITED BY
BILL GILLARD & ROBERT STAUFFER

BOOK PUBLISHING COMPANY
RHINEBECK, NEW YORK

Paperback ISBN 9781958972953
eBook ISBN 9781958972960

Library of Congress Cataloging-in-Publication Data

Names: Underhill, Evelyn, 1875-1941 author | Gillard, Bill (Professor)
editor | Stauffer, Robert, 1965- editor
Title: Then may the senses fall : Evelyn Underhill's forgotten fiction /
edited by Bill Gillard, Robert Stauffer.
Description: Rhinebeck, New York : Monkfish Book Publishing Company, [2025]
| Includes bibliographical references.
Identifiers: LCCN 2025017440 (print) | LCCN 2025017441 (ebook) | ISBN
9781958972953 paperback | ISBN 9781958972960 ebook
Subjects: LCSH: Underhill, Evelyn, 1875-1941--Criticism and interpretation
| Short stories, English | Fantasy fiction, English | Horror tales,
English | Christian fiction, English | Mysticism--Fiction | LCGFT:
Fiction
Classification: LCC PR6041.N6 T44 2025 (print) | LCC PR6041.N6 (ebook)
LC record available at https://lccn.loc.gov/2025017440
LC ebook record available at https://lccn.loc.gov/2025017441

Book and cover design by Colin Rolfe

Monkfish Book Publishing Company
22 East Market Street, Suite 304
Rhinebeck, New York 12572
(845) 876-4861
monkfishpublishing.com

CONTENTS

INTRODUCTION

English mystic and theologian Evelyn Underhill (1875-1941) is regarded primarily for her groundbreaking and accessible studies on Christian mysticism. She wrote over forty books and hundreds of articles, essays, and lectures on spiritual practices, including her most famous work, *Mysticism* (1911). As a young adult, Underhill sought far and wide for a connection with God and with inner peace. She chronicled some of that work in the speculative stories and poems that make up the book you are reading now. And yet despite her worldwide renown as a leading figure in Christian mysticism, these short stories and poems have been almost totally neglected. This collection serves to bring these excellent and intriguing stories back out into the light.

What's in This Book

This collection contains a mix of short fiction, poems, and a single essay, all written during what we consider to be a critical period for Underhill. We assert that Underhill's brief creative career represents an important step in her mystical and spiritual development. In other words, understand these stories and you go a long way toward understanding how Underhill became the transformational thinker and mystic the world knows her to be. Created in the decade before her massively popular *Mysticism*—the book that made her famous among the mainstream reading public—these stories and poems allow us to experience her transformation from wanderer and independent scholar to historian and defender of Christianity. They can be read as her travelogue of the ineffable world as she was experiencing it.

Five of the stories collected here were published in 1905 in *Horlick's Magazine*, an obscure and short-lived advertising periodical for a malted milk company. One also later appeared in our book, *The Spark of Modernism: Twenty Speculative Stories and Writings That Defined an Era, 1886-1939* (2023), a fiction collection that we edited with James Reitter. "At the End of the Garden," exists only in manuscript form in the King's College London archive. It is published here for the first time. The final story in the collection, "The Threefold Quest," was published in *The Treasury*, an illustrated magazine published in London, in 1907. We know of no other short fiction written by Underhill as an adult, although some of her juvenile stories remain uncollected.

We have included several poems chosen from Underhill's books *Immanence* (1912) and *Theophanies* (1916) because they serve to illuminate and deepen the themes that we see in the short stories. There is no sure way to know the dates of composition for these poems, but many of them appeared previously in the journals such as *The Quest*, *The Nation*, *The New Weekly*, *The Westminster Gazette*, and others. We imagine them as thematic and likely contemporaneous complements to the stories with which we chose to pair them.

We close our collection with her essay, "A Defence of Magic" (1907), because it explores her understanding of the permeable frontier between the spiritual and mundane worlds. The influence of the secret societies and Underhill's friend, the mystic and author Arthur Waite (1857-1942), are seen here quite clearly. Her connection with the European Continent and facility with language are also on display. Most important, perhaps, is that the essay is evidence that her growing Christian convictions were part of a gradual evolution in her thinking that can be seen most clearly in the stories and poems that make up the bulk of the collection. Underhill's fervent desire to reconcile her Christian faith with her experiences of worlds beyond is what lies at the heart of her mystical teaching and at the center of all of the writing here.

You may have already noticed in the table of contents that we've included brief commentaries on each of Underhill's creative pieces included here, labeling them "outros." The word is used most often in music, where the "outro" is the concluding section of a song or composition. It's also used to describe the closing credits in a film. We chose to comment *after* each piece so that you, the reader, may share the joy of discovery of these stories without an editor getting in the way telling you how and what to think about a particular aspect of the text. We also limited our commentary to a narrow slice of the text; the outros act as impressions rather than comprehensive textual or thematic analysis. We hope that this matches the spirit of these strange and wonderful stories, that in our groping in the darkness for a way—not the only way—to understand otherworldly and mystical events the characters experience shows you one possibility for finding depth in what are fascinating pieces. The outros vary in length and scope and are decidedly optional reading. The real show here is the forgotten creative work of Evelyn Underhill.

The Journey to Mysticism

Although she is now honored on the liturgical calendar of Anglican churches worldwide, Evelyn Underhill was not always so confident about her place in the Anglican Church—or any church for that matter. The years when she was writing these short stories and many of her poems was a time in her life when she did not have a clear direction, a time when she was seeking a religious home.

Though she was baptized in the Anglican Church as an infant, a diary entry by the sixteen-year-old Underhill hints at an early ambivalence toward organized religion:

> As to religion, I don't quite know, except that I believe in a God, and think it is better to love and help the poor people round me than to go on saying that I love an abstract Spirit whom I have never seen. If I can do both, all the better, but it is best to begin with the nearest. I do not think anything is gained by being orthodox, and a great deal of the beauty and sweetness of things is lost by being bigoted and dogmatic. If we are to see God at all it must be through nature and our fellow men. Science holds a lamp up to heaven, not down to the Churches. (Cropper 5)

Her precocious tendencies as both a thinker and a writer are recorded in the correspondence she had with a local journal called *Hearth and Home*, starting in 1891. The journal is, as the title implies, a magazine for people looking for a well-ordered home, which discussed innovations and modern life. Most notably for students of Underhill, it had a page called "For Lassies and Laddies," which was mostly puzzles and clever information about the world for young people. Underhill's name appears nearly weekly among those who have successfully solved the puzzles, and she also appears in the letters to the editor. She even won a short-story writing competition that contains what must be her first publication, a short story called "A Literary 'At Home,'" about literary characters coming to life in the dreams of a young reader (*Hearth* 530).

Underhill's father, Sir Arthur Underhill (1850-1939), was a prominent lawyer and a devoted yachtsman, who taught his daughter to sail and travel. His primary work was on torts and estate law. In his autobiography, *Change and Decay: The Recollections and Reflections of an Octogenarian Bencher* (1938), he mentions his daughter only to note that he did little of significance in the 1870s except marry his wife and have a daughter come into his life. He mentions his son-in-law, Hubert Stuart Moore more often, but only in his recollections of yachting. Sir Arthur's influence on Evelyn can be seen in her first publication, a collection of poems and songs centered on the law entitled *A Bar-lamb's Ballad Book* (1902). Her thoughts, while ever driven to spirituality, seemed to have found a good foundation in her father's firm grasp of the law.

Underhill's developing spiritual sensibility was further molded during her journeys to Europe with her mother during the end of the nineteenth and beginning of the twentieth century, particularly throughout France and Italy. These adventures are chronicled in her notebooks and sketchbooks, parts of which were edited by her friend Lucy

Menzies in a posthumous book called *Shrines and Cities of France and Italy* (1949). These sketches and letters show an artistic side to Underhill, a talent matched with her interest in book-binding. They also hint at Underhill's growing perception of two worlds: one of mundane everyday life and another that she labels "Reality," a mystical dimension that is hidden from everyday eyes but which surrounds us at all times. This is an idea that would become a fundamental tenet of her later and much more well-known writings on mysticism. On these trips, she encountered Roman Catholicism directly, and her many sketches reflect her growing interest in that tradition. The intense spirituality she found in Catholic architecture and in sacred art affected her on a level she had not yet found in the Church of England. She began to seriously consider converting to Roman Catholicism while at the same time writing the short stories contained in this collection.

In 1907, when she turned thirty-one, Pope Pius X sparked an argument between Modernism and Roman Catholicism when he denounced, most notably in the papal bull "*Pascendi gregis*" (1907), the approach Underhill was beginning then to take toward a mystical understanding of religion. This conflict dismayed her. At the same time, she faced a different kind of pressure to abandon interest in the Roman Catholic Church. Her fiancé, Hubert Stuart Moore, expressed concern that the sacrament of Confession would come between them as husband and wife. Underhill explained: "He insists [...] that all hope of our happiness is at an end, that he could never again trust me, no more mutual confidence possible, that there will always be a priest between us" (Cropper 30).

Even more important than her personal relationship

with her husband was her broader concern about the Pope's attitude toward the changing times:

> I no more like the tone and temper of contemporary Romanism than you do: it is really horrible; but with all her muddles, she has kept her mysteries intact. There I can touch—see—feel Reality: and—speaking for myself only—nowhere else. Alas, you won't approve of all this, and I don't either—it is all wrong, but at present I don't know what else to do. The narrow exclusiveness of Rome is dreadful—I could never believe it, for I feel in sympathy with every Christian of every sort—except when they start hating one another. But to join any other communion is simply an impossible thought. (Underhill *Letters* 126)

Torn between her fiancé and Roman Catholicism and also by Pope Pius X's encyclical against Modernism and her own desire for an intellectual pursuit of religion, Underhill found that she could not commit to Christianity in any form just yet.

We include "A Defence of Magic" in this collection because it represents for us an exclamation point to this period of Underhill's spiritual life. By then, she had spent the previous few years developing her mystical theology alongside such writers as Arthur Waite and Arthur Machen (1863-1947), but she was still seeking for a way to reconcile this new way of thinking with her Christian roots. She was also voraciously reading newly recovered texts at the British Museum thanks to her friendship with the librarian, J.A. Herbert, who introduced her to the then-unattributed *The Mirror of Simple Souls* (fourteenth century); Underhill would never know, as we do now, that the author of this work—that had such an impact on her own—was Marguerite Porete. Herbert also introduced her to Richard Rolle and Walter Hilton, two other English hermit-mystics of that century.

In his biography of Underhill, Christopher Armstrong explains her connection to the idea of Magic, a word she routinely capitalizes in "A Defence of Magic," as an attempt to show a consistency between her return to Christianity and her dalliance with a secret society in Great Britain dedicated to the study and practice of metaphysics and occult Hermeticism. Underhill recognizes that her desire to connect with the unseen world had taken her down some strange paths, but not so strange when she considered the origin of Christianity and its rituals. Armstrong writes:

> [I]n these pages Evelyn takes up and defends the course of a man such as Lévi who, as she saw him, began with "a form of intellectual curiosity," was led on through magical practices to "a mystic seeking of transcendental truth"; then passed on to a conscious and elaborate exploitation of artistic, conceptual and natural symbols; came to an understanding of compassion and the abiding value of suffering freely accepted; and finally brought the whole story to an evidently exemplary climax by becoming reconciled to the Roman Catholic Church to which he originally belonged. It is difficult not to read another story into this, the story of Evelyn's own career (Armstrong 44).

Armstrong asserts that Underhill found a sympathetic character in Alphonse Louis Constant (1810-1875), better known by his pen name, Éliphas Lévi Zahed, the French esotericist, poet, and writer. Underhill does talk about such a spiritual path in her first novel, *The Grey World* (1904), and is so clearly drawn to the idea of a Seeker of Truth who has to travel the whole world before concluding that the answer was right there all along. However, Armstrong does seem to miss one step in that process: the ecstatic communion that begins the whole quest. He sees it as intellectual curiosity but never asks on what it might be based.

Underhill describes in "A Defence of Magic" how Lévi experienced in his education a moment that remained unexplained to him. When he held a sword during a ritual in which he was to summon an angel who would answer his questions, he felt a tingling sensation in his shoulder, which led him to collapse into a coma. When he awoke, he felt that his questions had been answered.

A similar event happened to Underhill in 1907—the year she published "Defence" and the year she was married to Hubert—when she visited a friend at a Franciscan convent and had a "vision" which converted her back to Christianity, specifically to Roman Catholicism. Charles Williams, in his introduction to a volume of her collected letters, notes that she wrote about it in her diary on February 4, 1907, but seems to have not fully processed it until she wrote again about it on May 14, 1911 (Underhill *Letters* 13). Perhaps this is what linked her to Lévi and her desire to write "Defence." In *The Grey World*, Underhill describes the hero's memory of the life in that unseen world that he experiences in between his two lives in the seen world. The intellectual curiosity comes from a moment of ecstasy in which the unseen world is penetrated, even if only for a moment, and so, perhaps, her fiction presaged her own visit to the unseen world.

During the next decade, Evelyn Underhill would

produce many nonfiction works on mystics and their writings, including her seminal works, *Mysticism* (1911) and *Practical Mysticism* (1914). These works connected her intellectual curiosity, begun in her search through the secret societies and magical studies, to the institutional Christianity that would come, in time, to revere her. She never again, as far as we have been able to tell, attempted to express her ideas of the ineffable through fiction. Even her poetry would not continue, except as prayers, after 1921, the year she reconsecrated herself in the Anglican Church. She was then forty-five years old.

In the time between the wars, Evelyn Underhill became well known for her spiritual guidance as a retreat leader at her beloved Pleshey, an Anglican retreat center forty miles northeast of London, and for her search for more practical versions of mystical ideas and practices. In the last two decades of her life, Underhill taught on mysticism, meditation, and the search for God in both conventional and nonconventional places. She led hundreds of retreats at Pleshey and corresponded with many who sought her aid in their own attempts to find peace in a contemplative life. She became one of the most well-known Christian mystics of the twentieth century and earned a permanent place in the annals of the Anglican and Episcopal churches worldwide.

Literary Mentors: Machen and Waite

Arthur Waite and Arthur Machen had a profound influence on Underhill's growth both as a creative writer and as a philosopher and mystic. Machen was a well-known actor, journalist, and storyteller who often wrote about mystical realms, most notably in "The Great God Pan" (1894). His view of the hidden world was different and more horrifying than Underhill's. In his work, he showed the importance of society, in particular religion and ritual, in keeping at bay that terrifying realm. His influence can be felt in the horror literature of the twentieth century, notably in the legacy of H.P. Lovecraft and his disciples.

During this critical period for Underhill, she also developed a relationship with Arthur Waite, the co-creator of one of the most well-known versions of the Tarot deck. Waite helped Machen to revive his fiction output by encouraging Machen to write new stories for his fledgling *Horlick's Magazine*, a publication filled with malted milk advertisements that was distributed in the Asian and Australian colonies of the United Kingdom and lasted for just two years. Waite was the editor of Underhill's short fiction, including all five of her stories that appeared first in *Horlick's* and are now in this collection.

Waite, Machen, and Underhill were members of the secret society that had begun as the Hermetic Order of the Golden Dawn. There are some discrepancies about the years in which Underhill participated in the Order. Armstrong indicates she might have been a member as early as 1903, and was still there in 1905, as evidenced by a few letters to Arthur Waite (Armstrong 36-37). Charles Williams indicates that she began her time with the Order in 1904 and stayed for several years (Williams 12-13). If *The Grey World* reflects Underhill's experience with the Order, it is true that she did not find her affiliation with it completely satisfying. In her novel, Willie Hopkinson meets up with a group, the Searchers of the Soul, which is made up of intelligentsia all trying to use magical rather than mystical approaches to see "beyond the veil":

> With knowledge lying so close to their doors; with the emblems around them of an unstable, impermanent world, which he knew to be ready to rock and dissolve at the first blow dealt upon the portals of sense; with phrases on their lips which constantly touched the edges of the Truth; it seemed incredible that these people could continue so profoundly earthly, so desperately dense, making game in their happy ignorance with the secret beyond the veil. (*Grey World* 50–51)

Willie, perhaps reflecting Underhill's experience, perceives the whole thing as foolish and shallow.

Underhill's creative writing, including the novels, *The Grey World* and *The Lost Word* (1907), seems to be strongly influenced by Waite's poetry. His poem, "The Grey World," which appeared in Waite's *Strange Houses of Sleep* (1906), describes the waif that seems to match in all but gender Underhill's protagonist in her novel of the same name. Waite's play-poem "The Lost Word" is about the crumbling house of a character named Widow who seems to represent the rigid and conservative Roman Catholic Church. In Underhill's novel, *The Lost Word*, the architect of a new church finds a divine inspiration for his artistic endeavors and must let go of his earthly bonds—a growing affection for one of the other artists—in order to finish his great edifice. Both Underhill and Waite address how the power of God can no longer be found in the ancient notions of the church but must now be found in openness to new thinking and experiences. Beyond this, we can only speculate as to the nature of the friendships Underhill made with Machen and Waite because of the paucity of letters and other evidence that have been preserved.

We are certain that Underhill published five of her

short stories in *Horlick's Magazine*, a curious place indeed to find nearly the entire short fiction output of a writer who would go on to great fame. What exactly was *Horlick's*? James Horlick's dream was to create a superfood that would end the daily tedium of deciding what to eat. He almost got there: he created a nutritious powdered milk that could be shipped to colonial troops all around the world. Arthur Waite served on the board of trustees for Horlick's company. Somehow, either as a commission or as a brilliant idea of his own, Waite became the founding editor of *Horlick's Magazine*. Waite writes of his accomplishment in his memoir, *The Shadows of Life and Thought:*

> As a fact the review lasted for fifteen issues and was then abandoned, not because sales were on the downward grade but because the periodical was not selling as it should. I had edited it with utmost care and had secured a few contributions which belong to literature at its highest, from Arthur Machen as well as from Evelyn Underhill, whose repute as a mystical writer is at present second to none among living people. (167)

The contents, which featured many of Waite's own pieces published under a great variety of pseudonyms, included works by Robert Lynd and Edgar Jepson, who would also become prominent writers. He published Machen's stories, particularly "The White People" and the "Garden of Avallaunius" (later titled "The Hill of Dreams") both as serials over five issues, and Underhill's five short stories. Machen would go on to republish his works that appeared in the magazine, but by that time Underhill found herself already branching off into her new career as scholar of the medieval mystics.

Underhill's Short Fiction Legacy

The major theme that runs through all of the stories and poems here is that humans are extraordinary spiritual beings living in an ordinary world, and that it is the clash of these two truths that challenges us in our faith and in our dealings with one another. Underhill's short stories are full of artistic and spiritual beings who must find a way to live with the problems of mortality—the need to eat, sleep, protect ourselves from the elements, and so on—while continuing their spiritual journeys. Her artists inhabit a realm beyond the veil where they catch haunting glimpses of truth and reality while at the same time needing to make a living in a mundane world that is often hostile to visionaries. Her artists must reconcile their desire for depicting the reality they see and the kind of art that most people want from them. In these stories, even Nature itself holds the key to the great sacrifice that lies at the heart of Christianity.

Arthur Machen wrote a review of Underhill's third novel, *The Column of Dust*, in which, despite the fact that the book was dedicated to him and his second wife, he calls it a failed experiment:

> We can hint at the unseen world, we can symbolise it, we can trace it, as it were, the shadow of it thrown upon this solid earth of ours; we can see the image of it "per speculum in aenigmate"—through a glass darkly; but—and this is a very great but—we cannot incarnate the unincarnate. Miss Underhill has done her very best; she has done, indeed, exquisitely; but being mortal, she has not succeeded in putting on immortality. (*Mist and Misery* 78)

This sentiment might just as well apply to her short fiction. Like Machen, Underhill often tries to show the intrusion of the unseen world on what humanity has dubbed the real world. In some cases, her protagonists are there to protect more ordinary people from this intrusion. In others, the protagonists are trying to understand what they see themselves, battling the disconnect between what they expect of the world and what it really gives them. In the end, either the individual must accept the fact that their experience is not the experience of everyone else, or they must suffer for their attempts at depicting or explaining what they see to an unreceptive audience. Truly, Underhill is describing the role of the prophet, at best, and the martyr, at worst. It is nearly impossible to exist in both the seen and unseen worlds and maintain the rationality human beings like to call reality.

Each of the seven stories attempts to give the reader a glimpse into the world beyond without drifting into a fantasy world, as George MacDonald did in his *Phantastes* (1857), and without the horror of Machen's "Great God Pan." Underhill's stories are not about extreme heroes doing the impossible and encountering the Godhead directly. She attempts to show the reader how the profound enters life in the quietest and subtlest of ways. One needs only to open one's eyes to see the miraculous world.

The stories and poems in the collection are Underhill's first attempts to explore the ideas about the mystical. In the next decade, her fully mature understanding arrived in *Mysticism* (1911) and *Practical Mysticism* (1915). Mysticism does not belong only to the desert fathers who could spend their days outside of civilization studying ancient texts. Connection to unseen mystical worlds can be found also by humble parish priests, artists, and, really, anyone who is willing to fully open their mind to it.

We hope you enjoy Underhill's travelogue of the ineffable!

THEOPHANY

(*Immanence* 35)

Deep-cradled in the fringed mow to lie
And feel the rhythmic flux of life sweep by,
This is to know the easy heaven that waits
Before our timidly-embattled gates:
To share the exultant leap and thrust of things
Outward toward perfection, in the heart
Of every bud to see the folded wings,
Discern the patient Whole in every part.

* * *

Outro: Underhill's Many Theophanies

A theophany is a physical manifestation of God to a human. There are theophanies throughout classical literature; two of the earliest examples are from *The Epic of Gilgamesh* and *The Iliad*. There are many examples of theophanies in the Bible, for example, including manifestations of the Abrahamic God to Moses, Joshua, David, and Elijah, among many others. In Christian Orthodox tradition, Theophany is a holy day celebrated in early January. Arthur Waite had a much more traditional definition of the word in his poem, "Theophany" (1906), where he limits the manifestation of God to a single event in Bethlehem that is chronicled in the New Testament.

In chapter 7 of *Practical Mysticism* (1914), Underhill builds upon the ideas of ninth-century Irish philosopher and theologian, John Scotus Eriugena. Eriugena wrote that the many manifestations of life that humans encounter in our world indicate the whole, the omnipotent God, behind the variety:

> I should believe that by that name [Nothing] is signified the ineffable and incomprehensible and inaccessible brilliance of the Divine Goodness which is unknown to all intellects whether human or angelic—for it is superessential and supernatural—which while it is contemplated in itself neither is nor was nor shall be, for it is understood to be in none of the things that exist because it surpasses all things, but when, by a certain ineffable descent into the things that are, it is beheld by the mind's eye, it alone is found to be in all things, and it is and was and shall be. Therefore so long as it is understood to be incomprehensible by reason of its transcendence it is not unreasonably called "Nothing", but when it begins to appear in its theophanies it is said to proceed, as it were, out of nothing into something, and that which is properly thought of as beyond all essence is also properly known in all essence, and therefore every visible and invisible creature can be called a theophany, that is, a divine apparition. For every order of natures from the highest to the lowest, that is, from the celestial essences to the last bodies of this visible world, the more secretly it is understood, the closer

> it is seen to approach the divine brilliance. (Eriugena 307-308)

Eriugena's ideas about theophany shine through in Underhill's poem in words and phrases that emphasize the humble, multiplicity of everyday theophanies. For Underhill, the manifestation of God was not Waite's rare or biblical event. On the contrary: there were theophanies happening everywhere, every day. In each of them, this poem suggests, anyone with awareness might "Discern the patient Whole in every part." In Practical Mysticism, Underhill explains it like this:

> You have begun now the Plotinian ascent from multiplicity to unity, and therefore begin to perceive in the Many the clear and actual presence of the One: the changeless and absolute Life, manifesting itself in all the myriad nascent, crescent, cadent lives. Poets, gazing thus at the "flower in the crannied wall" or the "green thing that stands in the way," have been led deep into the heart of its life; there to discern the secret of the universe. *(Underhill Practical 97)*

THE DEATH OF A SAINT

Father John had earned the title of saint by years of white living and fervent piety. He was greatly beloved; for he had always contrived to be radiantly holy without any unpleasant insistence upon virtue, and lacked that air of obtrusive unselfishness which is so irritating to the moderately good. He was old—not very old; it was said that he aged prematurely, from abstinence. His very keen dark eyes, which made the sweetness of his smile seem a paradox, were ensigns of a fretting sword within.

He was dying now: serenely, without struggle, but also without ecstasy. It seemed as though he were the last person to be interested in his own departure from life. His stillness gave dignity even to the bare and comfortless bedroom; bare, not with the interesting, ecclesiastical plainness of furniture bought for austerity's sake, but with the dull and rather squalid dreariness of cheap, ugly things grown old—of painted deal washhand-stand, rep curtains, a faded pattern of drab daisies on the wall.

There were a good many people in his room; neighbours

whom he had helped and encouraged to be happy, and especially the two young men who lived with him. They had been his pupils in priesthood and good works; and he, who was humble in most things, had allowed himself to be proud of them. The one whom he called Alban, his white Roman, sat now on the edge of the bed and watched his master's face—not anxiously, but as one participating vicariously in a great joy. He felt himself truly to be less the victim of a terrible bereavement than a disciple whose high privilege it was to be associated in the passing of this exquisite soul. The other pupil—his name was Cuthbert—was much occupied with medicine bottles and the smoothing of bedclothes. He was a tall, strong young man with a round head and a good temper. His noticeable common-sense blurred the outline of his other virtues; and Father John, whilst praising the methodical habits which made him the prop of the household, had formed the habit of calling Cuthbert his right hand, but Alban his son.

So these two tended the sick man; the thoughts of the one intent upon his body, the thoughts of the other keeping time with his soul.

The room was very quiet. The neighbours who had come in watched the bed dumbly, with awkward affection. They came for the most part from a class which is expert in death-bed etiquette; but this quiet departure confused them. A sense of petition was in the air, but inarticulate. No one dared pray, though the moment asked for it; they all felt like amateurs in the presence of a great artist. So they remained silent, shuffling their feet; and Father John slept.

It was very early in the morning, but the event which they waited for took their thoughts to a place where time is not counted any more: so that the striking of the church clock brought into the uneasy stillness of the room a noise almost supernatural in its sharpness. Everyone, half consciously, counted the seven strokes. Father John opened his eyes, and saw the people who watched him. They came nearer then, every one secretly hoping for a word of personal farewell. They loved him; and loved still better their belief that he loved them.

He raised himself up in the bed, and stared at them; but not with the gentle gratitude that they had expected.

Then he said, abruptly "Are you here because I am dying?"

No one answered. For a short time he considered them in silence. Then, in a very clear and peremptory tone, he said, "Go home!"

They were immensely astonished; and because they were astonished, perhaps a little because they were accustomed to obey him, they went—all but Alban and Cuthbert, who stayed, and watched him as before.

Father John did not speak again. He had relapsed amongst the pillows, and lay still; unconscious, apparently, of his nurses, of his own inappropriate conduct, of everything but some strong and secret thought which was dominating his mind. He gazed straight before him, with an expression that seemed first an effort to remember, then an effort to understand, then an intense anxiety. He was looking at the door in the wall opposite to his bed. Alban and Cuthbert were silent, fearing to interrupt some sacred meditation. They knew all which that door meant to him: and whilst Cuthbert dreaded its effect upon his temperature, Alban was grieved that it stood between his soul and a serener light. Its key lay under his pillow, for it was always kept locked. He raised his hand presently, feeling for it; and the hand fell back helplessly, refusing duty. At that, a look which was almost terror came over his face. Alban knew, in a quick gust of understanding, that the saint's heart was set on opening that door once again before he died.

Every morning at seven o'clock he had gone through it alone, locking it behind him: and at ten o'clock had come out again as though strengthened for the day—peaceful, joyous, eager for good works. No one but himself had ever passed that threshold, but everyone recognised that beyond it lay the secret of his saintship. Alban liked to think of him there, alone before his little altar, prostrate perhaps, wrestling in the spirit and receiving divine consolation. The hours spent in that room were, he knew, the determining influence in Father John's life. He had often seen him go in depressed and nerveless, almost morose; to come out, after three hours of silence, serene and ready for the world. Alban himself, noticing this daily miracle, tried to spend these hours in prayer and meditation; but suffered much from wandering attention, and was unable to assure himself of any decided result.

But now it was evident that the closed door was a torment, not a joy, to the dying man. He looked at it with a fixity of desire, and apprehension of his helplessness, that were fast becoming an agony. He raised himself a little and Alban bent to catch his whisper.

"I must go there," he said. "Must. A duty—undone—I can't leave it."

Cuthbert said to him very gently and sensibly that he might now leave earthly duties to the care of his sons; that soon Paradise itself would be his oratory. But the saint, for the first time since they had known him, forgot to be grateful for kindness.

"I can't die like this, it's horrible—impossible. Must go in." He had struggled now to a sitting position; his pale, thin face was convulsed by effort and anxiety.

The two young men, who could not understand his pertinacity, felt helpless too. Alban wavered; he had so long made Father John's will his own that the idea of opposing him seemed unnatural. But Cuthbert, upheld by his own knowledge of nursing, merely put a firm arm round the patient's shoulders and forced him to lie down again; this was not the moment for foolish scruples about the demeanour of youth towards old age.

Alban whispered, "Dear Father, your prayers will be heard wherever offered."

Father John paid no attention to Alban's remark. He shook off Cuthbert's detaining hand in a sudden spasm of strength, and they saw with amazement that he was angry—the black anger of a strong-willed man who meets with a sudden check. He said with surprising and unsaint-like directness: "Young fools! It can't matter what a dying man does. I must die; but to die with this undone would be a sin. Can't you see that I mean it? Help me up."

Cuthbert fetched a dressing-gown without speaking; there was, indeed, nothing to say, for his action was involuntary and inexplicable. Together he and Alban helped the patient from bed and across the room to the closed door. They reached it at last, very slowly and with difficulty; for even that dominant will could not steady the dying limbs.

The last trembling steps were almost too eager. He nearly fell upon the threshold, but clung to the doorpost, and holding that, motioned them away with an extraordinary imperiousness. So supported he could stand alone. They moved to the far end of the room, abashed by his so evident anger and the difficult responsibilities of the moment; and from there they felt, rather than saw, that he did somehow contrive to unlock the door, went in and shut it behind him.

It was Cuthbert who ran immediately and put his ear to the keyhole, explaining the act to Alban as a sacred duty.

"He may faint, or even die," he said, "So weak, no vitality left, and the room must be cold. We ought never to have allowed this; but it's done, and we are bound to watch over him. If he dies there, we shall be to blame. You could see that he is scarcely answerable for his actions."

So they waited silently in the bedroom, which seemed suddenly to have become large, empty and terrible. All of life, for them, was behind the closed doors. They listened, their tense nerves reporting every irrelevant sound, as if it were a trumpet call; so that they heard each other's breath, and the rattle of the ill-fitting window in its sash, each as a separate horror. But from behind the door they heard nothing. They felt frightened and responsible, yet incapable of interrupting that last devotion which a dying man was determined to offer with every accustomed ceremony to his God.

Alban had crept to Cuthbert's side, and his ear, too, was against the door. Presently they heard slow, heavy footsteps; then a longer, duller sound.

Alban whispered, "He is kneeling."

Cuthbert answered, "I am afraid he may have fallen, he is very feeble." His voice was husky and uncertain; the closed door had already begun to have its effect upon the nerves.

There was silence for a little while; then a low moan, scarcely more than a sigh.

Cuthbert said, "I'm certain he has fallen: we ought to go in."

"No. He forbade it," answered Alban.

He stopped, for Father John was speaking, "My God! have mercy, have mercy! I can't do it," he said; and then another moan, very low and bitter. "Too late! No strength."

They waited a long while after that, but the silence was not broken again.

Eight o'clock struck. Cuthbert said: "He has been there an hour now. I know we ought to go in: it is murder to leave him."

Alban answered: "He may be in ecstacy; and to break that would be a sin."

He felt it to be something worse than murder that Cuthbert's medical attentions should intrude upon that holy hour.

They waited for a short time longer.

Then Cuthbert said, "I can't help it, I must call him." He felt faint, chilled, and shaken by the silence and anxiety.

They spoke Father John's name several times; and there was no reply.

Then Cuthbert suddenly rose to his feet, and without speaking to Alban put his shoulder to the locked door, and threw all his weight against it. Alban, without any definite idea of his own action, found himself helping; and together they pushed silently, careful not to meet each other's eyes. The door gave way almost at once. It was old and slight; and had, indeed, availed less than the honour of his disciples to keep Father John's refuge shut from the world.

The door, therefore, broke open abruptly; and almost before they were aware of their own breach of faith, the two young men went in. They had expected an oratory; perhaps made beautiful with the fruits of self-denial, perhaps as drearily insignificant as the bedroom, yet certainly filled with that secret magic which invests any place set apart for communion with the unseen.

What they saw was so different and undreamed of, that it temporally obliterated from their consciousness the old man whom they had come to find. They were in an artist's studio. Not such an artist as those whom Father John had always loved deeply, and helped with special words of practical counsel and wise encouragement—the painters of visionary landscape, stern, holy Madonnas, or peasants ennobled by their work. This was the workshop of a great painter; but his subjects were the grotesque, morbid, unspeakable secrets of the world. Papers were pinned to the wall, or lay in heaps upon the floor; and on each was the impression of something evil and alive—a matter of a few strokes, mostly, but in some cases finished with a care that approached the act of creation. The things were male—female—no sex—always human, but always bestial too. In all, a spirit breathed, and in all a likeness was visible. It was Alban who first saw with terror that the likeness was to Father John.

In the same moment Cuthbert gave a cry, and moved quickly to the far corner of the room, where an easel stood by the window turned towards the light. There was a shapeless mass on the ground before it; they stooped, recognising its shabby draperies. It was Father John, quite dead. There was a paint-brush in his clenched hand.

Above on the easel, a picture faced them with an air that was almost defiant. It was the most horrible of all the pictures in that horrible little room, and seemed to gather up into itself the unnamable evil which the walls distilled. Painted with a technical perfection which they were not able to appreciate, it pulsated with life, laughed cynically at its own monstrous suggestion; passion had created it, and it lived. In it were personified all the dark, obscene secrets of our common nature. That riot of horror whose symbol is the Bacchanalia, was present here in its foulness and strength; and again the face of the protagonist was like the shadow of the face of Father John.

The paint upon this picture was scarcely dry; it glistened in the light. It held their attention with authority even while their master lay dead at their feet. A subtle change was worked in the room which it now commanded. Some evil ferment had been poured out and was already at work. Both young men lost immediate sense of reality, as happens to those who step abruptly beyond the edge of their own universe. Cuthbert became excited. His eyes shone, his hand trembled; his lips were parted in a sudden, cunning, understanding smile. Unexpectedly he was drawn out beyond himself towards these pictures, which roused some creature dormant within him. The pictures spoke to this creature as to a fellow-citizen; and Cuthbert perceived with joy that he was alive—a man.

Alban was dazed and dreamy. He was trying to fit this studio and its inhabitants into his pious concept of the world.

Presently Cuthbert went nearer to the picture, looking especially at one passionate and emaciated face which stared from a cloudy corner. A broad, uneven streak of black seemed half to obliterate it, and ran waveringly to the other side of the panel, a meaningless disfigurement of the design. Within an inch of the edge it stopped, as if the hand that drew it had failed suddenly. Cuthbert, on an impulse, touched it. It was quite wet.

They looked then at the saint, and at the brush in his hand, still fully charged with the same dark pigment.

Cuthbert laughed—the assured laugh of a worldly and incomplete comprehension.

"He came here to destroy these," he said.

"Then for us," replied Alban, "they are destroyed."

He went to Father John and raised his head. Cuthbert went to the feet, and together they carried the body back into the bedroom, and laid it on the tossed and dingy bed. Alban knelt by it, but Cuthbert had turned back hastily and stealthily, and stood at the studio threshold again. He knew himself to be standing at the threshold of Destiny.

Before him was an offer of inconceivable pleasures, but behind him the weight of Alban's character made itself felt. It had the strength that belongs to ignorant innocence; so that presently it happened that Cuthbert drew back, vexed but conquered, and quietly propped the broken door in position as well as he could, placing a chair against it for greater security. He did not wish the neighbours to see those studio walls. Then he returned to Alban, who still knelt by the bed; stooped over him; and touched his arm. He had again become Cuthbert, the wise and reasonable friend.

"Well, well," he said, "It's a queer world, full of surprises; but who would have expected this? Our saint was only an artist after all!"

But Alban did not answer. He remembered with tears that Father John had always come from that room purged from the stain of earth and radiant with thanksgiving; with a heart, now stilled for ever, which had longed to help and comfort all the world. It seemed possible that, had he been less of an artist, he might not have been quite so much of a saint.

* * *

Outro: Visions of the Other World

Evelyn Underhill's biographer, Christopher J. R. Armstrong, dismisses "The Death of a Saint" as just a bit of derivative fun. He parallels it to Emile Zola's *Therese Raquin* (1868) and Oscar Wilde's *The Picture of Dorian Grey* (1890) (Armstrong

45). But Armstrong's analysis comes up woefully short when considering the immense depth and complexity of Underhill's story. This is no "mirror" story, as Armstrong would have it. Father John's secret room is not where he confronts some secret shame that he hides from polite company. Instead, "The Death of a Saint" stands out among these seven forgotten stories because of its connection to a genre that had not yet been invented, but was on the brink of lurching to life.

"Cosmic horror," as defined by H.P. Lovecraft in his landmark essay, "Supernatural Horror in Literature" (1927), contains:

> [a] certain atmosphere of breathless and unexplainable dread of outer, unknown forces must be present; and there must be a hint, expressed with a seriousness and portentousness becoming its subject, of that most terrible conception of the human brain—a malign and particular suspension or defeat of those fixed laws of Nature which are our only safeguard against the assaults of chaos and the daemons of unplumbed space. (Lovecraft)

Lovecraft uses as examples work by Ambrose Bierce, Edgar Allan Poe, and Arthur Machen, among others, but he might have also included this strange story by Underhill, had he known about it. It contains many or, perhaps, even all of the elements that Lovecraft was speaking about when defining this slice of weird fiction.

In many ways this story exists between Arthur Machen's "Great God Pan" (1894) and Lovecraft's "Pickman's Model" (1926). Machen's story offers a scientific explanation of how the brain has developed locks which keep out the unseen world in order to protect our own sanity. Dr. Raymond thinks he is giving his test subject, a young girl, a great gift in allowing her to see beyond "the dreams and shadows: the shadows that hide the real world from our eyes" (Machen "The Great" 218). Instead, he gives her only madness. Lovecraft's "Pickman's Model" describes a painter of surpassing genius who paints horrific scenes. He depicts the terrors he has glimpsed beyond the veil, unspeakable visions unseen by most.

"The Death of a Saint" shows readers the role Underhill sees for saints; they are the brave ones who bear witness to the ineffable. Underhill asks, What do we do when the saints inevitably fail, as the old priest seems to in Underhill's story? Should good people strive to fully open their eyes even if they risk becoming insane like Mary in Machen's story? Or should people play it safe and simply allow themselves to return to the polite fiction of mundane reality?

CLOUDS

(*Immanence* 11–12)

Why should the angels list our tiny life?
The drama of the cloud is theirs to know:
Great loves and hates, much pageantry of strife,
Vocations various as the winds that blow.
Swift savage living things with streaming hair,
Maternal presences that slowly move
On the curved meadows of the upper air
Where freckled flocks athwart the pastures rove:
Ceaseless they come and go,
The travail of the Spirit to declare.
That which to us is cloud, perchance may be
The massy landscape of Reality.

I think the angels lean from out their land
As children round some pool upon the shore,
That with a rapt and glad amazement pore
Upon the many-coloured magic deep;
Nor guess the myriad wonders of its floor
Because beneath the bannered weed they creep.
So looking, they behold
Our little patch of ribbed and pebbled sand

All set about with silver, fold on fold;
And hardly seen
The jungle-life of branching cloud between
Which fills the middle-ocean floating free.
Upon its tide
Those great unfettered populations ride;
Theirs is the glory of the world, and we
Are but the creeping things deep drowned beneath that
sea.

So, upward gazing to the epic sky,
Perhaps we meet the angels' brooding look:
And we and they within it may descry
Some mutual book
Wherein they read
The long liturgic office of the earth,
As we upon the other page may find—
Meet for our lesser skill—
In the diurnal language of mankind,
A Gospel and a Creed.
News of the Will
That gave us birth,
A Gloria for our mirth,
And an ensample how we may ordain
The strange and stormy pageant of our pain;
That beauty's solemn mood
Attend the dreadful breaking of the flood,
And grace, as rain,
Fall from that sacrament to help the arid plain.

* * *

Outro: The World Within "Worlds"

"Clouds" has that strange moment when angels, who are perched on their celestial pastures that, to us, seem like clouds, gaze down at humanity as if staring into the mysterious depths of the ocean. Meanwhile, humans look up with little understanding and no effective tools by which to communicate with such creatures.

The poem posits a common language and "[s]ome mutual book" that would allow both to converse in some superficial way. The incomplete knowledge that humans are able to gain along the way is rain falling from those clouds like a "sacrament" upon our "arid" lives. It is the idea of finding a common language with the angels that is so interesting in this poem.

In *Practical Mysticism*, Underhill laments the inability of language to express anything other than our humdrum existence. It is as if the greatest poets can write nothing but shopping lists. Witness here the quotation marks around the word "world" in the first sentence, a word that could, in many other contexts, have an obvious and uncomplicated meaning:

> From the transitional plane of darkness, you will be reborn into another "world," another stage of realisation: and find yourself, literally, to be other than you were before. Ascetic writers tell us that the essence of the change now effected consists in the fact that "God's *action* takes the place of man's *activity*"—that the surrendered self "does not act, but receives." By this they mean to describe, as well as our concrete language will permit, the new and vivid consciousness which now invades the contemplative; the sense which he has of being as it were

helpless in the grasp of another Power, so utterly part of him, so completely different from him—so rich and various, so transfused with life and feeling, so urgent and so all-transcending—that he can only think of it as God. (Underhill *Practical* 128)

THE IVORY TOWER

The Ivory Tower is set in the midst of the sea, and very few people have seen it. In the town that is at the edge of the ocean there is always a certain talk of it; and on clear days a sudden cry will come that one or another has found it on the horizon. Then the citizens run down on the beach, as far as they can without wetting their feet, and they strain their eyes and lose their tempers in the effort to assure each other that they have really seen the tower. But for all that, the honest ones go home unconvinced; and presently the life of the city goes on again and the tower becomes a common-place of conversation.

It lies west of the land that is known; and a princess is in it. She awaits her lover, her rescuer, with inconceivable gifts. She is lonely and beautiful, for in her is all the secrecy and all the loveliness of every woman in the world. For the people of that city all mystery, all faëry, and all joy are hid in the tower. It is said to be white, tall, and shining; and those who would reach it must take ship and follow the path of the Western Light.

Now and then some eager heart arises in the city who is determined on the quest of the Ivory Tower. It is the dread of all mothers lest this longing should wake in their boys. Therefore they make haste to marry the dreamy and adventurous lads to girls of the city and so secure them; for they find that the torch of the wedding always puts out the fire of the quest. Then the boys become useful citizens like their fathers, and breed up children to inherit their dead dreams; only when the cry of hope comes from the shore they remember, and run to the edge of the water to look for the Ivory Tower.

Nevertheless, it has happened that some have set out on this adventure. They have gone alone, for this must be the way of it; but none have achieved the end. Many things have happened to hinder them; for being solitary in their boats in the midst of the ocean, the sea has whispered to them with a thousand voices, the land has sent after them a thousand regrets, and they have been able no longer to look steadily in the path of the Western Light. So it has happened that they thought they saw the Tower to the north or the south, very far away yet evident; and they have turned from their course to search for it. Then they have wandered for many years, finding nothing; and some have died at the helm, and some reached cold and foreign lands, where they have stayed fearing worse fate; and a few have at last returned home, old, weary, disheartened.

And others there have been that sailed always westwards, till at last they came to a great and perilous rock that stood in the path of the Light. Some deflected their course for it, and passed to the north or the south; and these sailed on and on, finding nothing, for they had not been true to the way. Others, more faithful, chose to run headlong on its ledges, trusting their dream. These perished miserably. The face of that rock is stained with tragedy, and its foundation is strewn with wreckage. Those who are in the city fear it, for they know that it is always waiting to seize upon their sons.

Now once there was born to a woman in the city a boy more than ordinarily full of wild audacities and gentle dreams. He came out of due time, for at this period the people of the town were of a practical mood. They wisely judged that the tower which none could find, and its legend which none could prove, evidently belonged to an earlier stage of their culture. In those days if anyone cried out that he could see it, his friends smiled and spoke of his imagination. There was no excitement in the city, no sudden rush towards the shore. The people had started manufactures, and were very content to develop the land that they had without searching for less tangible riches on the sea. Their ships of adventure were dismantled; one or two of the more picturesque patterns were taken to the museum.

Then this child came. He was a boy who always held his head high and looked upwards, because, he said, the sky was so much prettier than the ground. He annoyed his relations very much, for he was always treading on their toes. When he was yet very little, he heard the story of the Ivory Tower; for now it had dropped from the plane of faith to that of fairy tale, and was greatly esteemed by children. This boy loved it, and he saw always in his dreams that Desirable Princess, and the Ivory Tower that stood westwards below the horizon. He walked constantly by the sea edge to look for it: and watched and watched, for he knew that there were moments when it might be apprehended. And at last it happened that one evening he watched the sunset from the top of a very high cliff that lay south of the town. It gave him a great view of the world; he saw the ocean, dreadful, formless, eager for adventurers, and the path of the western light that lay across it. And far away, where that light ended, he suddenly perceived the Ivory Tower standing in the midst of the sunset. He saw it clearly; dreamy, magical, but very distinct, shining like a pillar of white fire against the flaming skies. And the path of the Western Light began at his feet like a riband of gold, and led over sea to the foot of the tower; straight as a shaft to the home of the hidden Princess.

A voice within him said: "You are called to the Quest." From that moment, for him as for his fathers, all mystery, all faery and all joy were hid in the Ivory Tower.

On the next day he took a boat and began to provision it for the voyage. His relations did not hinder him, for he was a very useless person, and they had always expected him to do something that would justify contempt. They said:

"Where are you going?"

He answered: "In the path of the Western Light."

Then they laughed, and some were sorry for him, seeing that he suffered from delusions; for at this hour of the day the pathway was not visible. The sun was about his business in high heaven, and the doors of his palace were shut.

They said: "Poor fellow; he means the sunset."

And his aunts and his uncles reassured one another, saying: "Better let him go. It is a nice calm day, and he will soon come back. He never had much perseverance."

But they did not know that he had a compass to keep him in the path when the light had left it, and a certainty of the achievement that waited at the journey's end.

So, without many farewells, he set out and steered westwards. He was leaving the comfortable for the adorable, the known for the unknown. For so great an undertaking his departure seemed quiet enough; but then, no one believed in it. He knew that the voyage would be a long one. Therefore, though he soon lost sight of the city, and no other landmark rose on the horizon; though all day the waters seemed pathless, and he never saw the tower, he was not dismayed. Every evening, when the path of the Western Light appeared upon the water, it lay in golden ripples round his boat, and he knew that he had not missed his way. Sometimes the seas were rough and difficult; and it seemed to him then that he fought with dancing flames, and was wet through by watery fire. But still he sailed on and on, for he knew that the road was right, and that all his joy was before him.

Once, after many days, he thought that he saw the tower far away in the north; but he remembered the sunset vision, and kept his prow pointing west.

Sometimes when he was tired and weak the voices of the sea said: "You are deceived; we hide nothing, we lead to nothing. There is no quest and no end, only eternal wandering in the cup of the waters under the infinite sky. With dreams of the tower we spread the net for our victims, but the only fulfilment is death in our arms."

But he did not hear them, for always he looked upwards away from the impermanent waters. The sky cried: "Go on! There is another fulfilment." And every evening the sunset brought him a reminder of his pathway and fresh hope of the Ivory Tower.

And after a very long time, when he had lost count of the weeks and forgotten the days in which cold hunger and thirst were not permanent features of life, a storm came up from the east as night fell, and his boat was driven before the wind at a great speed through the darkness. Very soon he lost control of the helm; but he did not mind that, for his compass told him that he was still in the path of the west, and he believed that every wave he breasted brought him nearer the journey's end. So he shortened sail and lashed his tiller, and sat in the bottom of the boat waiting for the wind to abate and the day to come.

At last, when he had tossed for many hours in an unchanging world, only measuring the darkness by the pale light on the crests of the oncoming waves, each so like the other that all sense of progress ceased, a blacker darkness rose in front of him. It was a great and smooth rock that stood right in his path. Then he knew that he had come to the peril which wrecked so many adventurers, and kept so many cowards from the quest. But he would not turn from it if he could, for it barred the path of the west; and for fear the back wash of the sea should sweep him past it, he unlashed his tiller and steered straight for the cliff. And a breaker took him and cast him upon it, so that his boat was entirely destroyed. But he had hold of a piece of wood that supported him, and presently he was washed against a crevice of the rock and there found foothold till morning came. He was wet and weary, and full of despair; for now that his boat was gone he knew that his journey was done. The sea murmured to him all night, "We hide nothing, we lead to nothing; you are alone in the cup of waters under the infinite sky." He felt very small and helpless, and wished for death.

Now when it was light, and he could see the place where he was, he perceived himself to be on a ledge at the base of the cliff. The sea was quiet, and the waves no longer reached him; but they watched him, he thought, like animals waiting impatient for their food. All about was the wreckage of ships that had come on the quest; the ribs of them covered with barnacles and weed, the rusted ironwork, the tattered glories of their hulls and wings. He saw fragments of his poor boat also. On the face of the cliff and at the base of it were the stains of the gluttonous sea.

But when he had seen all this and realised afresh his own solitude amongst it, he looked up towards the light, as he was accustomed to do: for, however evil the world might be, the sky, he knew, was always lovely. Then he saw above the brown and sea-worn cliff, which was all the lost adventurers had ever seen, a white and shining wall that rose spired and battlemented into the highest heaven. The morning light hit it and transfigured it to a citadel of snow. He had come to the Ivory Tower, for it was one with the perilous rock: he knew that behind that wall the Desired Princess was waiting, and in her heart all the secrecy and all the loveliness of every woman in the world. And with her was the achievement of the quest.

Now his weariness left him, and all his misery, because of the joy he had that his failure was turned to success: and he climbed up from the ledge where he was, and went from crevice to crevice, and from crag to crag, wading in the surfy water, till at last he stood under the western face of the tower, where the wrecks had never come. There it was, white and beautiful from the summit to the water's edge, as he always dreamed it to be. High up on that western face he found a locked door, and steps cut in the wall that led up to it. There he climbed, and knocked, and waited.

And after a while he heard footsteps within the tower, and presently the door began to open very slowly, on hinges that groaned as if being wakened from long sleep. When it was wide open he saw a very old woman, who stood upon the threshold looking out. She was thin and shriveled; her blue eyes looked faded and tired as if she had been watching the sea for many years. But he was eager for the princess, and did not notice her very much.

He cried out "Where is she?" and she answered, "Here."

She stood aside and let him pass her; and so he entered the Ivory Tower. He found a very bare and desolate house, for all its beauty was in the light that played upon its walls. He went into every room, and they were all empty. Then he came back to the old woman who had received him, and whose pale and weary eyes had watched him as he went to and fro through the tower.

And he said to her very imperiously: "Show me the Desired Princess." For indeed he felt that she kept him unjustly from his joy.

She answered: "Do you not know me?"

He said: "Not you!—not you!"

She replied: "Have I not had time to grow old whilst I waited for my lover? I have been here since the beginning of the world; yes, and before the world was, for I am older than God and more difficult of access, and you are the first that has knocked at my door. None who are solitary can be young, and I am the most lonely thing in all the world."

He turned his back on her, for he was full of anger at the thought of the things he had suffered and the mockery he had found. And he said: "You lie! for it is known that all faery, all mystery, and all joy are hidden in this tower."

She said: "Yes, and ever will be for the dwellers in the city and the adventurers on the sea. Had you stayed there with your dream you had desired me still. You are grieved against me because now I show myself to you as I am; but I cannot help it, for you sought me deliberately, and those who will seek must find. I cannot deceive you with that which is not, for my name is Truth. All men desire me because none have seen me. Because of that desire you thought me beautiful; but no achievement can ever be as beautiful as the quest.

When he heard her he wept, for he was bitterly disappointed.

Then she said to him: "Shut your eyes." And when he had done so, she put her arm about him and kissed him very gently.

Then, indeed, he felt in his arms that which he had sought; all the secrecy and all the loveliness of every woman in the world. And he knew that he had found that Desired Princess whose kisses are sweeter than her lover's hopes.

But whilst she still held him blinded and joyful, so that he thought this was indeed the truth, and all that went before had been the dream, she led him to a mirror, and said: "Open your eyes and look."

And when he had done so, he saw a very old man and a very old woman who stood side by side. They both had white hair and weary faces, and their eyes were pale with long watching.

When he had looked, he whispered: "Am I old?"

She answered: "Yes, for you have found me, and youth cannot do that. Many boys seek for me because they do not know me; but when they come near all the powers of the world strive with them, for fear they should find me and lose their youth. Then they turn aside, and some are lost and some go home. Your childhood was over in the moment when you steered straight for the perilous rock; but whenever you would have it again you need only refuse to look at me. He who knows how to shut his eyes can always find the desired princess."

Then he hid his face in her dress, and said, "Oh, Truth, blind me for ever, for I had rather love than know."

And because she is compassionate, and knew that he had sought her faithfully, she did as he asked; and he loved her, and had great peace. For indeed there is no better fate than this—to lie with dim eyes in the arms of illusion and dream that truth is beautiful and the Ivory Tower an attainment worthy of the quest.

Now, I do not know how it was, but somehow a part of this tale, though not all of it, has come to the ears of the citizens at the edge of the sea. For this reason belief in the Ivory Tower has come back into fashion; and though, perhaps, the old fervours have got rather sophisticated, they have again made it the home of all mystery, all faery, and all joy. None of the present generation have seen it yet, but their theories on the subject are very instructive.

* * *

Outro: Love Was Our Lord's Meaning

In "The Ivory Tower" we can see the strong influence Underhill's own quest for the "unseen world" had on her work. She was still a few years away from putting her research all together to write her *Mysticism*, and she was just finding her way back to the Christian faith.

By 1904, Underhill had already rediscovered the works of Marguerite Porete (though she would never know that Porete was the author of the book she uncovered), Julian of Norwich, Jan von Ruusbroec, and so on. She had written several pieces for local journals and community magazines. She had even begun gathering stories for a book she would publish in which she collected medieval miracles surrounding the Virgin Mary. But she had not found what she was seeking among either Anglican or Roman Catholic churches. "The Ivory Tower" seems more of a chronicle of her journey through the less canonical Christian beliefs such as theosophy and the mystical practices she found in a secret society like the Hermetic Order of the Golden Dawn.

In *Mysticism*, Underhill would attempt to describe the ineffable Trinity of God the Father, the Son, and the Holy Spirit by breaking it down this way: a) Light; b) Life; and c) Love. Her descriptions of this three-fold path is reflected in this story. She refers to God the Father, as an "Uncreated Light" that is always there, ready to be seen by anyone who has eyes to see. In her section about Life, she refers to the Son as the "hidden Steersman of the Universe" (115). In her story she describes a brutal travel, wearing out the seeker, turning him old and worn by the time he reaches his goal. A journey is an easy metaphor for life, specifically the contemplative life, as the hero in this story travels alone following a light that is not always visible to him and yet somehow always leading him onward.

Underhill, encountering works like *The Mirror of Simple Souls* about the time of the writing of this story, notes that there are many who die in the shipwrecks at the foot of the lighthouse while our hero is able to continue the journey into the lighthouse to find the Desired Princess, a representative of the last of the Trinity, Love / the Holy Spirit. In Porete's *Mirror*, a distinction is made between those who simply seek the promised land and those who enter it and become part of it. Even finding the Source of Light is not enough; one must continue on into the Tower.

One must leave behind earthly senses in order to find the desired: "He who knows how to shut his eyes can always find the desired princess," she tells the traveler. In *Mysticism,* Underhill writes, "Proceeding according to Christian doctrine, from Light and Life, the Father and Son—implicit, that is, in both the Absolute Source and dynamic flux of things—this divine spirit of desire is found enshrined in our very selfhood; and is the agent by which the selfhood is merged in the Absolute Self" (117). This story then describes not only the mystical journey to obtain the light of understanding, but also to suffer the harshness of life and the ends of desire.

SUPERSENSUAL

(*Immanence* 16–17)

When first the busy, clumsy tongue is stilled,
Save that some childish, stammering words of love
The coming birth of man's true language prove:
When, one and all,
The wistful, seeking senses are fulfilled
With strange, austere delight:
When eye and ear
Are inward turned to meet the flooding light,
The cadence of thy coming quick to hear:
When on thy mystic flight,
Thou Swift yet Changeless, herald breezes bring
To scent the heart's swept cell
With incense from the thurible of spring,
The fragrance which the lily seeks in vain:
When touch no more may tell
The verities of contact unexpressed,
And, deeplier pressed,
To that surrender which is holiest pain,
We taste thy very rest—
Ah, then we find,
Folded about by kindly-nurturing night,

Instinct with silence sweetly musical,
The rapt communion of the mind with Mind.
    Then may the senses fall
Vanquished indeed, nor dread
That this their dear defeat be counted sin:
    For every door of flesh shall lift its head,
Because the King of Life is entered in.

* * *

Outro: The Spiritual Sense

A "thurible" is a metal container into which incense is placed and burned; the openings at the top of the container release the smoke while the thurible is swung from side to side suspended by a chain. It is an integral part of the rite of both the Anglican and Roman Catholic Mass, and as such is a physical representation of the connection between humans and their God. Underhill explores this idea in *The Mystic Way* (1913), divining humanity's relationship with God:

> [I]n the Divine Liturgy of the Orthodox and the Mass of the Catholic Church, this ceremony is the great living witness to—the great artistic expression of—those organic facts which we call mystical Christianity: the "transplanting of man into a new world over against the nearest-at-hand world," the "fundamental inner renewal," the "union of the human and the divine."[1] All the thoughts that gather about this select series of acts—apparently so simple, sometimes almost fortuitous, yet charged with immense meanings for the brooding soul—all the

[1] Euchen, *The Truth of Religion*, pp. 544-545 [Underhill's footnote]

> elaborate, even fantastic symbolic interpretations placed upon these acts in mediaeval times, have arisen at one time or another within the collective consciousness of Christendom. Sometimes true organic developments, sometimes the result of abrupt intuitions, the reward of that receptivity which great rituals help to produce, they owe their place in or about the ceremony to the fact that they help it in the performance of its function, the stimulation of man's spiritual sense; emphasising or enriching some aspect of its central and fundamentally mystical idea. (Underhill *The Mystic Way* 336-337)

The thurible in this poem is not the incense vase of Roman rite. Instead, it is the "thurible of spring," something resembling the tool of worship but arising from the non-human realm. In this poem, human senses fall away as one by one they are revealed to be inadequate. Their fall, the poem contends, is the necessary step toward the activation of "man's spiritual sense" and an eventual (re)union with the King of Life, whose arrival ends the poem.

THE MOUNTAIN IMAGE

Nicholas was born a proud dreamer. He was arrogant before men, for his art's sake: humble before his art, because he knew that he had betrayed her. He worked all day in the small open shop which gave on to the village street, and dreamed all night of the marvellous and adorable things that he had not been able to do.

The village was the prettiest in the valley: pretty with the quaintness of tiles and painted woodwork, not of insanitary decay. In the summer many visitors came to it; and they all stopped before Nicholas' shop and praised the dexterity of his carving with loud cheerful voices which rasped his nerves. They bought all the things that he most despised himself for doing, and ordered more of the same kind—figures of girls in lace veils wonderfully imitated; plump babies; groups of mountain oxen, the affectionate cow with her calf, the heifer chewing the cud.

Their demands kept Nicholas' hands busy, so that the beautiful shapes he dreamed of remained the exclusive property of his soul: and the block of white marble which he had bought with his savings when he was a very young man remained in its corner at the back of the shop. When he left his apprenticeship he had promised himself that he would carve from this block a great Madonna, which should express his faith, his vision, the best of his art. No sentimental, maternal figure, but a divinity instinct with the austere loveliness that haunted his dreams. But first, he said, he would perfect himself by the study of meaner models, the making of little human things. It seemed too great a presumption to attempt the highest with an unskilled hand. No one had told him that this was his only chance of attempting the highest at all.

Years went by, and he remained amongst the meaner models: held captive first by their difficulty and then by his own cleverness, which brought him a constant stream of clients. So he relapsed into the facile reproduction, for money's sake, of the things that at first he had taken as an exercise to train him for the true work of his life. But every night, when he had put away the little figures of peasants and animals, the laughing masks that the tourists thought so wonderfully artistic, and all the rest, he saw in a vision severe and beautiful shapes, great solemn images waiting to be freed from the marble; and he knew that he had betrayed his gift and prostituted his dream. He grew morose; detesting his own horrible facility, hating the praise that he got from his neighbours, dreading the silent contempt of the art that he had deflowered. He gave his customers what they wanted with the careless impatience of a man tossing bones to a dog, and turned his back on them when they congratulated him on the beautiful finish of his statuettes. They thought him ill-mannered but very clever, and ordered more dancing peasants and pastoral groups. It sometimes happened, when he was alone in the workshop, that he went to the far dark corner and kissed the old block of marble with tears.

One summer, when Nicholas' reputation was well established in the valley, and his trade was at its height, the old sculptor who had taught him his craft came to pay his pupil a visit. He was past work, and lived now with his grandson at a distant farm, where he spent his time very happily cutting terminal heads upon the gate posts with his knife.

The old man came into Nicholas' workshop and looked round. He picked up several of the statuettes and carried them to the light; turned them about, ran his hand over their curves. He seemed pleased with what he saw.

"Very nice, neat work," he said. "Pretty work. I hear the visitors like it. You will die a rich man, Nicholas. I am very glad to find you of so practical a mind. I was afraid, when you left me, that you were going to be a failure; you fancied yourself an artist, do you remember? Wanted to do big statues. Big statues don't come out of little villages; I see you have realized that. This talk of art has ruined many in our trade; but you are quite safe from that danger now. You have established your own style of work. No fear of your leaving it; your customers won't let you do that."

When the old man had left, Nicholas put away his tools. He could no longer bear the society of the little figures that were ranged round his shop. They seemed to be repeating the horrible phrases of his master's professional praise; saying, one after another: "You have established your own style"; "You have a practical mind"; "No fear of your becoming an artist now." They sickened him. He had never before acknowledged to himself that it was indeed too late; that the veiled goddess had turned from him for ever.

He looked out into the homely and comfortable street. Two fat peasant children were rolling in the dust, with some hens and a puppy. Opposite to him was the bakery, where a cheery woman, who regarded him as the most prosperous tradesman in the place, sold him his bread every day. Beyond were other cottages, and the gabled inn, and a general shop full of groceries, haberdashery, and clumsy china. It all wore a deadly air of permanent comfort. The village, no less than his customers imposed his future upon him. He wondered how it was that his proud hopes had ever come to birth in such a place. He could not match that secret dream of his against its solid common sense.

He looked up from the Village to the hills, which stood very clear and blue above its roofs. They, he thought, had no part in the stifling prosperity of the valley. They were proud, cold and pure, like his dream. They would welcome it, help it. In the hills, one could only carve greatly; he suddenly felt convinced that only in the hills could he make actual the visions of his secret love. They imposed high effort, just as the valley forced art to contribute to the petty comforts of daily life.

He looked at them with a greater attention. As the workshop now, after its many years of tyranny, repelled him, drove him out—so, at this moment, the hills took on for him a mysterious and positive magnetism. He remembered with longing one very solitary place in them, which he had found when he was a boy, rather unexpectedly, and had always kept in mind for some curiously suggestive quality of magic that it had. It was the highest point of the spur which ran towards the south—a spur made up of savage peaks and ridges, and great shoulders of twisted rock. Apparently inaccessible, at one spot it sloped up directly from the valley; first grassy, then steep, with loose stones and patches of whortleberry scrub—a hard and uninviting way, infinitely discouraging to the traveller.

Every foot of the climb, he remembered, seemed to take one further from humanity, yet no nearer to the journey's end. But suddenly, after hours of dreary effort, one stepped from the ascent on to a little plateau; a very tiny place, no more than the grassy threshold before a door. The door was there, too—the door of the mountain, closely shut; an immense and astonishing cliff which rose, augustly precipitous, from before the climber's feet. It was the crown of the range, and, as it had seemed to him then, the crown of the actual world.

He had felt this spot to be instinct with a secret and peculiar life, which had imposed itself on his imagination. There was an intense feeling of remoteness; a thing not always linked with mere distance of space. One looked down to the green and charming valley, dominated by the precipices of that lonely and gigantic cliff; and knew that the valley and its villages belonged to another and more kindly dimension, were filled with a different life.

Thinking of this place now, in the fury of helpless remorse that had followed his master's visit, Nicholas turned to the memory of its solitudes with sudden longing. There, set so high above the comfortable earth, he could work out his dream in peace. There, undisturbed by the praise, criticism or prudent advice of his friends, he might carve on the smooth face of that dominant cliff the mighty limbs of the Madonna whom he had so long seen in vision; express the ideal that had haunted his nights and poisoned the handicraft of his days. It was not too late. Only courage was needed, and a casting off of that detestable prudence which had won his old master's approbation. In a cleaner atmosphere, far away from those trivial figures and hatefully clever busts, it might still be possible to apprehend the veiled goddess and deserve her smile.

In the evening, he packed his tools, took food and a blanket, and left the village by the road that led to the hills. He was happier than he had been for many years; not hopeful, but sure of himself. He knew that he was going to serve art greatly, imprint his vision on the world. He was a proud dreamer.

In the morning he had reached the plateau on the mountain, and Dream had taken him altogether for her own. He looked up at the towering cliff, very smooth and grey, and planned the outline of the great Madonna he would carve there. She would be severe, chaste, and solitary; less the Mother of Mercy than the Queen of the World. Of so great a size as to be visible even from his distant village, he intended that she should possess this summit, and from it impose her law on the valleys below. The winds and the mountain spirits, he thought, would do her honour: more fitting servants of the Divine Beauty than the unlovely children of men. He collected boulders and built himself a rough staging, so that he might have access to all parts of the work. The loneliness of the place did not trouble him, for he was very busy—part workman, part artist.

When all the preparations were made, he took his chisel and mallet, and said a prayer before he struck the first blow. This work, which should make a sanctuary of the mountain top, and consummate the long-delayed dedication of his art, seemed to demand some ceremony of approach; an introit, perhaps, like that Song of Liberation which the spirits of the dead sang when the angel brought them to another and a holier Mountain.

It was on the third day that Nicholas began to acknowledge to himself that there were unexpected technical difficulties connected with this work. He was skilled in the handling of material. From the hardest stone to the most friable, he knew how to make it obey the touch of the tool. But this rock had curious properties that he did not understand: turned against him, deceived him. It seemed instinct with a spirit of perversity. The chisel would slip suddenly, making a false cut; a great chip would fly off where he least desired it, leaving the piece that he wished to remove untouched. Often, when he had done what he intended, the result was disappointingly ineffectual. He told himself that he could correct the errors as the carving went deeper, that with practice the difficulties would be overcome. The vision from which he worked was so clear before him that he did not fear any mistake.

But on the next day the roughly chipped outline of his figure appeared to him less definite, less severe than it had been the night before. He supposed that he had confused his dream with its accomplishment; but he felt, for the first time, discouraged, and even a little lonely. The cliff was so very great. The distance from the valley-life seemed infinite. The silence was unbroken.

On this day, the difficulties of the work were yet greater than before; the rock more recalcitrant. It seemed to him now that some violent influence was fighting against that image of the Madonna which he was trying to wrest from the stone. He grew nervous, and even imagined that invisible hands seized his tool and deflected it; that some living and inimical creature, hidden in the rock, was struggling towards daylight under his hand. When the evening came he had made no progress. The work looked uncertain and confused. He was exhausted and could not sleep, but lay with eyes wide open, listening for sounds. It was a very black night, and nothing broke the terrible silence.

He rose at daybreak and said a prayer as he went to his work. The clean energies of the new day reproached him for his nervous follies. Companioned by the sunshine and the busy hurrying clouds, he felt himself to be the master of his hill-top; knew that it depended on himself to impose whatever form he chose on the matter on which he worked. All that day he struggled passionately to bring the holy face of his Madonna into being on that hard and treacherous rock. Every hour he knew more and more surely that he was struggling against another force, not holy, but the dominant and resident power of that place. Sometimes, as the mallet fell, he fancied that he heard an answering blow in the heart of the cliff.

In the late afternoon, he gave over, wearied by the losing fight, and stepped back upon the plateau that he might see the rock face in entirety and judge the effect of what he had done. The features of the Madonna were blurred and indeterminate; her limbs indicated only by the convex masses which started from the roughly chiselled ground. But from behind the vague outline of her veil, he thought that another face looked out. The rock had flown from his chisel there in large, uneven chips. There was revealed in their place a dim and mocking profile, that strained passionately towards the light. It seemed to Nicholas that this face appealed to him for release, demanded his service. Whichever way he turned, its gaze followed and possessed him. He was seized then by a sudden passion of fear, feeling himself alone and surrounded by terrible secrets—some antique and natural sorcery against which the quiet religion of the valley gave him no defence—secrets of the evil rock that struggled with him, the awful face that looked to him for escape. The sky, too, was cold and dreadful; it ringed in the solitude of the mountain, cut him off from the safe and comfortable earth.

On an impulse, he rushed upon the cliff and struck violent and frenzied blows at the spot where that face had appeared. He worked with eyes averted, fragments of stone raining down from under his tool. When he looked again, it had vanished.

When he had slept and the day came again, he woke to calmness and strength. The evil sorcery had gone. He realised that he had been cheated by some chance configuration of the stone acting on tired nerves. He was disgusted by his own weakness; ashamed to think that so pitiful a fancy should have been allowed to obliterate his proud dream. He set to his task again and worked with real ardour, atoning by industry for his failure in manhood and faith. Steadily and quietly, from sunrise till dusk, he drove away the inimical rock, forcing the image of Our Lady out to the light. Day by day the work grew, and its growth absorbed him. It restored his self-respect.

At last the hour of completion came, when the final fold of drapery was finished, the final touch given to the fretted and pinnacled crown. Again Nicholas stepped back on the plateau to view what he had done. He saw the colossal figure of the Queen of Heaven, serene and majestic, enthroned upon the face of the cliff. But it was a dead queen that he saw; not the living divinity of unimaginable glory of whom he had dreamed in the years of low accomplishment in the valley. Here, in the mountain, far away from the stultifying influences of common life, he had hoped to fulfil that dream in all its grandeur. Yet here it seemed even less possible than it had been in the village to realize the holy image of actual loveliness. Something, he knew, worked against it; something that killed the divine child of the soul at its moment of birth.

In the little, vulgar workshop, surrounded by cheap statuettes, Nicholas had at any rate dreamed purely. But on this night he dreamed, not of exquisite visions or strenuous accomplishment, but of the strange, wild face that he had seen for a moment in the rock. It re-captured him now, for his work was done and his imagination was free. It seemed, he thought, to be appealing to him; tempting him, reaching out to him. It had power—an evil power. Against it his coldly perfect Madonna was helpless and inert. In its eyes shone the fire which burns in the heart of the mountain; that mountain whose virgin sanctuary he had thus invaded, violated to satisfy the arrogant claims of his art. Now, the spirit of the mountain turned on him. He lay in the grip of magical and inhuman passions; unimaginable presences stood by his side. He felt strange monsters stir within himself as he gazed in his dream at that dreadful and wonderful face.

When he awoke, he rushed to the cliff to look for her; but she was not there. Far down in the heart of the rock he thought that he heard mocking laughter. It was for him, if he dared, to set the laughter free. He knew that.

Then he looked up at his Madonna, so stern and so dead; and down into the sunny valley, a sane and ordered landscape of cornfield and copse. There could be nothing very evil in such a world; it was too bright, airy and benevolent. His terror left him. He remembered the experiences of the night with a certain aesthetic satisfaction.

Presently it occurred to him that the dream face, which he longed to drag afresh from the stone—the haunting and wonderful being whom, in his heart, he now passionately desired—might well be carved here, at the feet of the

Madonna. Some foil to her calm beauty might remove that sense of dead majesty which she now conveyed. A mountain spirit, crushed by her holy powers and acknowledging her dominion; her servant, as he had almost playfully fancied that the elementals of the hills might be when he first set out upon this work.

This, he told himself, would rob his dream of its evil magic, devote it to pious uses. It was a pity that so original a conception—a face all wildness and wisdom, the incarnation of the secret mountain life—should be lost to the visual world. But he knew that he lied; that in all the years of valley life his art had never been put to such vile uses as those he set her now. He was trembling with desire as he took up his tools.

It was strange that the rock, formerly so hard and recalcitrant, seemed on this day to obey every whim of his tool. Nicholas had never worked before with such brilliancy and swiftness; his chisel seemed to tear at the very heart of the cliff. Again he had the sense of invisible hands guiding the strokes; but this time they worked towards some definite accomplishment, not for the frustration of the design. Quite soon the first shadow of the tormenting face appeared, breaking out, quick and eager, from the prison of stone. But her air of appeal was gone now; she was dominant—a conqueror. The great Madonna looked curiously old, faded and ineffectual, beside the imperious vitality of her growing rival.

By evening the whole figure was done; and for the first time Nicholas saw the strangely perfect limbs, the ageless and exquisite body of the mistress of the hill. Freed from her imprisoning cliff, she stood as it were on the edge of the actual world, looking at it, in no sense a part of it: and still she had that mocking evil smile. Nicholas was feverish, possessed. He dared not touch his work, for fear the round limbs should move under his hand, or the writhing lines of the rock turn to hair. But he stayed beside her till it was quite dark, a captive to that tyrannous glance. When she was not any longer visible he lay down and fell asleep. He was very tired. He offered no devotion to his Madonna that night.

In the middle of the night he felt a warm hand touch his shoulder, and he started up to see that desired and dreaded face close to his own. She smiled; and now the smile was cynically triumphant. He understood that. She spoke; honied and unintelligible words. With those words the sense of the secret life of the mountains, which he had always apprehended in this place, rushed on him like a flood. A strange fire was lit in his veins. That hidden Panic Spirit which is in every artist's soul sprang to the light, demanding its mate. He leaped up from the ground that he slept upon, arms outstretched to catch her, hold her fast. And for one instant he did hold her—had the maddening delight of that shining and wonderful body, that immortal yet corruptible flesh, subservient to his will; that mouth which his act had brought into being laid close to his own.

Then she slipped from him, and he was alone in the darkness; staggering forward blindly, reaching out to find her again. An insane longing possessed him. He cried out to her, hoarse and helpless cries, as he tried to follow her swift and soundless steps.

When he saw her again, she was standing at the foot of the cliff. She appeared there before him, abruptly; her limbs white against the dark stone. He thought that she beckoned to him; that behind her the cliff opened for her passage; that she waited to lead him to some hidden city beyond the ramparts of the sensual world.

The dark spirit within him said: "There is joy, there is the satisfaction of all longing; there is the lost secret of life!" In the darkness the Madonna was not visible, only the white limbs and the mocking smile that paused at the door of the rock.

She drew back a step and beckoned to him again. He knew that if this time he refused her, she would never return. It seemed to him as if the whole life of the mountain stopped at that instant, hung poised in the balance. Only the dark Spirit cried, "On, on!" He sprang forward with all his strength: hurled himself violently upon her, as she vanished before him into the heart of the cliff.

There was a cry then, an awful cry of torment. The dream was over, and the proud dreamer had awoke. He lay dead at the feet of the mighty, but lifeless Madonna, whose carven knees had received the impact of his head.

That night there was laughter in the mountain.

* * *

Outro: Beyond the Ramparts of the Sensual World

There is a moment late in "The Ivory Tower" where the island princess says, "I have been here since the beginning of the world; yes, and before the world was, for I am older than God and more difficult of access..." It seems a curiously heretical moment for Underhill even at this moment in her spiritual journey. To suggest that there is anything older than God—the capital G shows that Underhill is talking about the Judeo-Christian idea of the solitary, omnipotent creator of the Bible—bumps right up against the idea that God has always been and always will be. A similar moment happens in "The Mountain Image," but not in so many words. The vision-driven sculptor is haunted throughout his life by the image of an impossibly majestic woman he believes to be a Madonna. He struggles to find the moment when his energy and expertise are at their maximum so that he can finally sculpt the Madonna of his vivid dream.

Underhill biographer Dana Greene argues that the story is primarily didactic, that the moral is that "to seek the perfect in and of itself, independent of the ordinary, and as an object of individual possession is to confront the demonic face to face" (Greene 19). More specifically, the sculptor resents his patrons, the tourists who purchase his carvings and make him a wealthy man, his old teacher who praises his work as "pretty" and "practical," and the overall lack of appreciation for true art that he sees among his peers. That he ascends a mountain to create his masterwork, that he intends to carve his Madonna into the face of an almost inaccessible cliffside, means that he has taken his idea of perfection outside of any useful social context. His pursuit is, as Greene asserts, for perfection itself and nothing more. But there is much more than simple hubris at work here. The sculptor is not making rational decisions when it comes to his vision. He is driven to the point of obsession in bringing his mystical vision to life under his chisel.

Just as the princess in "The Ivory Tower" claimed to be "older than God," this mountain spirit had been with the sculptor from the beginning. The problem is that for all of those years the sculptor had misinterpreted his vision. Just as so many Christian rites and beliefs are laid over much older religious traditions, the sculptor experienced a transcendent vision, one that would consume his thoughts and render all of his everyday life miserable. Then, because he is a Christian, he misnamed it a "Madonna" and attempted to make the vision conform to his idea about what it should be and what it might signify. His eye as an artist did not leave him at that moment, and he knew what he was seeing, although he could not explain why "[t]he great Madonna looked curiously old, faded and ineffectual, beside the imperious vitality of her growing rival." His final act that day was to "offer no devotion to his Madonna." In surrendering to the truth of the mystical vision, the sculptor abandoned Christianity to discover the true nature of the vision that had been haunting him for so long.

The violence caused by laying Christianity over a mystical vision of something outside of notions of traditional religion caused the sculptor a lifetime of disharmony and a quick death on a cliff face. Just like the intrepid sailor who landed on the island of the princess whose "childhood was over in the moment when [he] steered straight for the perilous rock," the sculptor's life had no more purpose, and yet his limited human senses lacked the strength to apprehend the true nature of the mountain spirit. To arrive at understanding, the sculptor is required to abandon all notions of the organized religion and its iconography into which he had tried to fit this irresistible vision. In their place, he embraces the ancient and unknowable being, one who, like the princess from "The Ivory Tower," seems to predate any human experience of organized and literary religion: "She appeared there before him, abruptly; her limbs white against the dark stone. He thought that she beckoned to him; that behind her the cliff opened for her passage; that she waited to lead him to some hidden city beyond the ramparts of the sensual world." As we find out, however, the vision is evanescent, and his headlong run to her embrace ends with a cracked skull.

The ending is not quite how the sculptor imagined it to be. He is dead and alone on a windy cliff ledge. The vision that drove him to obsession and madness killed him. It is the story of a failure to process an encounter with what lies "beyond the ramparts of the sensual world." Or is it? If the story ended with "He lay dead at the feet of the mighty, but lifeless Madonna, whose carven knees had received the impact of his head," we might be sure of Greene's reading, that the pursuit of perfection by fallible and weak humans is a fool's errand. But the story does not quite end there. What about that final sentence? Who is laughing? Is it more than one voice, filled with glee, having finally found the path to the true and real?

CELESTIAL BEAUTY

(*Immanence* 4–10)

Shy Heavenly Beauty peeps
The parted leaves between:
Hardly she may be seen,
So carefully her maidenhead she keeps.
The bold and roving eyes
That only seek for loveliness adorned,—
These, like a prudent maid,
She must evade.
'Tis for the wise
And gentle watcher, who upon the scorned
And common things of life delights to gaze
She keeps that magic moment of amaze,
When from her private lair
Sudden she does her plenitude declare;
And quick and wild
As a vehement child,
Enticed whilst still unsought, resigns her charms,
Nothing reserving, to her lover's arms.

Ah, beyond lot of men most fortunate,

Who takes shy Heavenly Beauty for his mate!
To him she whispers witch-like, "Dear one, come!
All earth shall be our home.
Come, come with me!
Where little living simple things you see,
There wells the primal fountain of our joy:
The furry bee,
The petalled meek delight
That folds the flower's dear secret from the sight,
New bracken-tips tight curled,
The radiance and the rain
Dappling with mystery the homely plain,
Clouds strangely white,
And all the accidents that wait on changeful light
To veil the substance of the shrouded world,—
These be our love's employ!

"Yea, and not these alone;
My touch from every stone
Shall strike strange fires, my breath on every rod
Shall make it burgeon with the life of God.
Even in the city streets
I shall declare my sharp intolerable sweets,
For all
The myriad shades and shapes of things are mine:
Where in the lamplight sepia pavements shine,
And the blue naphtha flames upon the stall,
Thence do I call
My lonely secret loud,
And weave my dread enchantments o'er the unseeing crowd."

Not only so:

But in the inexorable hour of woe
When the soul's self would faint,
With horror made most horribly acquaint,
Still at her lover's side shall Heavenly Beauty go.
In terror's last distress
When mortal loveliness
With dying life itself is seen to die,
When from the teeming earth ignoble mouths appear
To feed on that we worshipped: then, "My dear,
Be not afraid," she cries, "for *here* am I!
This darkness doth but hide
The intimate fair being of thy bride.
Yea, I am here!
With vile corruption's self I dare to stand,
And take my marriage-crown from out Death's hand.

"Stern was my schooling in high steadfastness:
The faithful consort of the Only Fair,
I in his footsteps went
Where none but Beauty and her God might dare.
I was the angel of Gethsemane:
Men say his comrades slept,
But I was there,
The altar of that agony to dress.
Mine was the art that spread
The starry tent
Above his royal head,
And mine the sigh that passed
Across the shuddering olives when he wept.
I ran before Veronica to cast
My cloths about his face, and took to me
The sharp and ineffaceable impress
Of Deity.

"Mine was the comfort, mine the mystic cup,
'Twas my twin-brother Pain outpoured the wine:
Our mutual care his crown
Did cunningly entwine
With branches from my secret rose-bush torn—
Earth's blossoming thorn
Of thwarted but unconquered loveliness,
The brows of my beloved to adorn.
Where Life was first struck down
Beneath the Tree,
There was I lifted up,
The hierophant of Life new-made to be.
I rent the veil; I thrust the eager lance
Straight to the living heart of all romance.

"Then swam the earth in darkness; I was seen
Of none
Since the world's light was gone.
Yet, in that dreadful night of utmost gloom
I kept my lonely watch before the nest
Men called a tomb,
Which I had builded for my darling's rest.
Mists were upon the garden; as the dawn
Lit the world's edge, it rose from tearful sleep
As if a shroud about its grief to keep
Against the prying eyes of the swift-pacing morn.
Mists were upon the garden! but between
The dew-drenched veils of Paradisal green
I saw the shape of One
Who moved soft-foot the living turf upon
With intimate quiet gesture of a friend.
'Behold!' I said
'The Gardener returns his little plants to tend.'

But, when he turned his head,
I knew that unto me was his desire;
Yea! as a sword of fire
Was Life within his hand, all ugliness to slay
That we might rule together o'er the transfigured day.

"Then I, that am chosen bride
Of the Eternal Wisdom, leapt from my lover's side
On wings of joy, his conquest to prepare.
I coursed the far world wide;
In the deaf ears of men I cried, 'Beware!
Lest Beauty's Lord should come whilst you are
unaware.'
I sang from out the sunset, in the trees
I whispered as a spiritual wind,
The many-coloured music of the seas
I made the meet expression of my mind.
Yet in all these
Those who had skill to see
My changeful features, hear my gentle laughter,
Would not discern the One who followed after
And touched my vision to Eternity.

"So, since I would not steal
The heritage of him I heralded,
Straightway I fled
The homely brake within
And hid my face and hushed my faery mirth:
Thence do I peep,
And watch mankind go walking in its sleep
About the bit of heaven it calls the earth.
Through the deep lanes
All feathery with the fragrant herbs that bless,

And pungent herbs that heal
Your little human pains,
They hunt, but never win,
Some final ordered dream of dreariness!

"Yet now and then
From out the ceaseless stream of sightless men
Comes one, wide-eyed,
And knowing to confess
In little things my sacred loveliness.
Then to his side
I leap from out my lair: I am his destined bride!
And quick and wild,
As a vehement child,
Enticed whilst still unsought, I give my charms,
Nothing reserving, to my lover's arms.
"And so it is,"
Says Heavenly Beauty in her darling's ear,
"That those who dwell with me shall never fear
Death's cold corroding touch;
Nor shall they miss
In life's extremity to find me near.
Nay, more; for such
As dare look deep
Within my fontal and mysterious eyes, I keep
The secret of another life than this."

* * *

Outro: A Perpetual Star

One odd moment in this poem occurs late with the reference to the "city streets" which become the realm of the divine just as more bucolic settings have served Underhill in other texts. Typically, in her poems and short stories, Underhill places access to the divine geographically outside of human society and far from the built environment. This poem is different. Somehow, the sacred intrudes upon the mundane:

> The effect of this form of contemplation, in the degree in which the ordinary man may learn to practise it, is like the sudden change of atmosphere, the shifting of values, which we experience when we pass from the busy streets into a quiet church; where a lamp burns, and a silence reigns, the same yesterday, to-day, and for ever. Thence is poured forth a stillness which strikes through the tumult without. Eluding the flicker of the arc-lamps, thence through an upper window we may glimpse a perpetual star. (Underhill *Practical* 118-119)

A clear dividing line between the tumult and distraction of human society and the possibility of a union with the spiritual realm is present in this excerpt from *Practical Mysticism.* "Celestial Beauty," on the other hand, offers no such clear delineation. This singular line stands out in Underhill's creative work of this period because it is so curiously different.

AT THE END OF THE GARDEN

Only an altruist could call it a duty to go and see old Farringdon: only a liar could call it a pleasure. Nevertheless, Harland, without probing the motives of his conduct too deeply, did feel impelled to look in on him now and again. He always felt irritable before going, and pleasingly benevolent afterwards. The thing, though he did not know it, had become a luxury to him. It made him realize how kind he was. The difficult hour spent in "making himself pleasant" to that arid and forbidding personality brought into sharp contrast his easy, sociable existence, his many interests, his wide popularity.

Farringdon had been his father's partner. "There should always be one disagreeable partner," old Harland used to say, "in every first class firm." Harland's father had not been disagreeable. He had accommodated himself to existence; had lived suitably, married suitably, died at a suitable time, and left his son a suitable income. Farringdon had done none of these things. He had contrived in some curious way of his own, to elude life: had never married, never had a hobby, kept a pet, or made a friend. Encased in his own crustiness, he seemed like a shell-fish that did not even respond to change of tide. Many years ago he had retired from a business in which his curious lack of humanity, his dull aloofness, had withheld him from success: and lived alone and apparently unoccupied in a steep old house at the top of a steep old square. Harland never knew how he passed his days, or adjusted himself to his own utter lack of interest in the world. His house, lifeless and stagnant, in which everything seemed some shade of grey or brown, was the predestined dwelling of a creedless tasteless anchorite of the upper middle class. Its walls were an effective shield against the assaults of human gladness and anxiety, of life light and love. Its windows were morose. Its passages exhaled sensations of solitude.

There was within it the dim stale atmosphere which comes from the lack of living emotions; not from faded wallpapers, drab and flattened carpets, or steel engravings set in heavy frames. The little straight garden tailed out behind it seemed like a strip of the ancient wilderness smeared with the by-products of the town. The very weeds cried *noli-me-tangere*. Farringdon's servants were as taciturn, as unchanging as himself.

Harland, then, returning to London after an agreeable summer holiday recognised with his usual sensation of annoyance that he "supposed he must look old Farringdon up." It was the act which symbolised for him the resumption of harness; the return to the monotonies, vexations, and responsibilities of urban life. He went at his usual hour in the late afternoon: for one did not lightly risk a meal in such a house. It had been a soft and misty October day without sunshine. With twilight came a clinging fog, and the raw breath of a rising wind. Climbing the square, Harland reflected, as usual, upon the disagreeable nature of the expedition: its futility, since Farringdon never seemed to find pleasure in his visits. Nature conspired with him to complete its horridness. He remembered that she had often done this before. Sometimes she had rained upon him with sullen appropriateness damping his spirits in advance. Sometimes she had met him with breezes as bitter as Farringdon's tongue. Sometimes she had made the afternoon radiant with a delicate loveliness: so that even the tarnished trees in the main road sent him invitations to all natural delights, and the prospect of a mouldy hour spent in Farringdon's library filled him with distress. It was also as usual that Elizabeth, the ancient parlour-maid, should open the door; and that Farringdon's dismal hall should still be unlit, though dusk was now come.

Elizabeth took his coat; and as she hung it up observed sharply and suddenly, "Mr. Farringdon's queer." The words gave Harland a shock that was at once immense and ridiculous. In the course of their long acquaintance-ship, he could not remember that he had ever known Elizabeth to volunteer a remark. He knew that it meant great things.

He replied, "Ill is he? I hadn't heard, I'm very sorry for that."

Elizabeth said again, "He's queer." She opened the door of the library: and Harland, entering, found that the room was empty. He wondered whether Farringdon's illness kept him in bed; what he would look like as an invalid, whether one would be asked to go upstairs.

Elizabeth anticipated the question. Her answer surprised him. "Down the garden plantin' bulbs," she said. Her voice had in it a tone of deep and resentful grief: almost of fear. It was the voice of one who speaks of dangerous and forbidden practices and expects therefrom the disintegration of her universe.

She went away, leaving Harland alone in the dusky little room. It was absurd, but her words had disturbed him profoundly. They had infected him somehow with her evident feelings of horror: her conviction that Farringdon must, as she said, be "queer."

There was no imaginable point of contact between the normal Farringdon, the Farringdon which 70 years of steady self-centered development and increasing isolation had produced, and the small and gentle flowers of the earth. One could not conceive his connection with the increase of beauty or life. Such discrepancies opened the door upon the grotesque; shook out of place the orderly arrangement of things. The picture of him busy with his trowel in that dismal flap of neglected garden, intent like any other mild old gentleman on getting in his crocuses before the first frost, was incredible, unnatural, horrid. It were easier far to conceive him with straws in his hair.

Yet the real Farringdon, when he entered the room, seemed normal enough. Only his fingernails advertised the occupations of the day. He was at once as correct and as ungracious as usual. If sanity depended upon a harsh and apathetic manner, it was too evident that his brain was still secure.

Harland said, "Elizabeth tells me that you have taken to gardening, sir."

Farringdon intimated that this was true. At the same time he made it clear to the visitor that Mr. Farringdon's "queerness" was not going to make the conversation any less difficult or more entertaining than usual. "Delighted to hear it. Jolly interesting occupation: healthy, too," said Harland. "You'll find it a tremendous amusement when the spring comes on."

Farringdon did not answer. His thin mouth closed sharply, and his guest received a subtle impression that the word "amusement" had been found insulting. The old man seemed to be considering some private business, far beyond Harland's range. The doors were fast shut as ever against all intruders: but now there seemed to be something behind them. Presently he said, as if to himself. "Must get the bulbs in before the end of October, if they are to have the flowers in good time."

"Quite, quite!" said Harland eagerly. "That' s the great point—before the ground gets cold. Crocuses, I suppose?"

Farringdon answered, "Daffodils—they prefer them."

"They'll be a nice show from these windows, if you've got them in the grass," said Harland. He loved flowers, and thought how piteous their pure radiance would look in such a place.

Farringdon replied in his harsh repellant voice, "They are all at the end of the garden."

"Making a little bulb-plot there, I suppose," said Harland, determined, if he could, to keep the languid conversation alive. Farringdon answered "yes," snarling the word, as if the confession were dragged out of him: and Harland ventured to observe that it was an excellent idea to concentrate on such a sheltered position.

"Anywhere else, they would have been useless," replied Farringdon curtly.

Harland thought this absurd; but felt it better that he should appear to understand. It was funny how this trivial business of the garden seemed to dominate them. It seemed impossible to talk of anything else: but of course when an old man breaks the habit of years and gets a hobby, it is apt to become an obsession, particularly if he lives alone. The gardening mania, however, had done nothing towards making Farringdon accessible. He seemed even more remote, more inhuman than usual: and Harland was glad enough when the ceremonial forty minutes was over and he was able to leave.

He had pity on Elizabeth's strained face, which awaited him in the hall; and said to her, "Mr. Farringdon seems well enough. I don't think you have any cause to worry."

She answered, "Well enough in his body. But he's queer, Mr. Harland, very queer." He wondered what she meant, but decided not to invite an explanation. One couldn't consult with the servants about old Farringdon's eccentricities. The idea offended his taste.

It was not until after Christmas that he again went to the house in the square. His own life was at full flood that autumn. Its stream overpowered the lesser interests which had filled his calmer days. He was in love; passionately, seriously, and—it was inevitable—selfishly. He had forgotten Farringdon: and it was only the sight of the forced daffodils in the flower shops as January waned that brought him suddenly to mind. A vague curiosity came then, to reinforce the usual sense of necessity which drove him to the house from time to time. He wondered what the old chap was doing; whether the gardening craze had been permanent, whether his "queerness," if it really existed, had increased. Seen in retrospect, eccentricities become interesting—even significant. That odd change in Farringdon, which he had found so tiresome, so disconcerting, now blended with the memory of Elizabeth's anxiety and the other, older queerness of the lonely stagnant house, to form an impression that was almost horrid. It suddenly seemed to ask for investigation:

pressed upon him as a responsibility, which he resented, but could hardly elude. He put it to himself that if the old man were really getting dotty—and after all dottiness begins in little things—it would be pretty awful for those two elderly servants, and he might have to see to things.

Elizabeth received him almost cordially. Mr. Farringdon was queer, she said, but very bright. Uncommon active he had been lately. He was down at the end of the garden. Perhaps Mr. Harland would like to join him there? He detected a note of appeal in her voice: and suddenly there came to him a conviction of some deep essential link between the garden and Farringdon's queerness. He remembered phrases in their last conversation that had struck him curiously as they passed: a necessity which seemed to brood over that sudden mania for gardening, fantastic rules which had to obeyed. There was a French window in the library: and a few steps led down to the gravel path. Harland, pausing at their foot, first thought that Farringdon's activities had contrived to leave the place unchanged. The rough and grimy lawn, on which every blade of grass emphasising the general baldness seemed a symptom of decay, the dismal little shrubs, the weed-filled beds fringing sooty walls, these were there in all their hideousness. But, looking about him for signs of human occupation, friendly care, he saw presently that a high trellis had been erected at some distance from the house as if by shaky and amateur hands; so that the end of the garden was now hidden from view. He reflected that this must veil the site of Farringdon's bulb-plot. It was like him to hide it away, out of reach of the general enjoyment. No doubt he was there now, tidying things up, admiring the results of his labours, doing unnecessary little jobs, in an old man's fussy way.

The path was sticky. Harland—always a natty man, and

now carefully dressed, for he was on his way to another and more interesting visit—went slowly, picking his steps with some care. When he was still a little distance from the trellis, he heard Farringdon's voice: talking apparently, to himself. The words were inaudible, but the tone astonished him; for it was the voice of a happy man, gentle and eager. One might almost have called it affectionate. It came to him in little detached fragments, with pauses between: as if the speaker were waiting for a reply unheard. Harland, listening to these amiable and unnatural accents, absorbed in his effort to distinguish their meaning, his growing amazement, forgot the prudent watching of his footsteps. He blundered at the corner of the lawn and struck his heel sharply against its tiled edge. At once, to his vexation, the voice ceased.

He reached the trellis, went round it, and met Farringdon, who came towards him with his measured, springless tread. His pale sunken eyes wore their ordinary cold and repellent expression. The corners of his thin mouth were drawn down. There was no welcome in his attitude; and Harland felt as though he had been detected in some indelicate act of intrusion. Farringdon, however, seemed less interested in this intrusion than in some object which lay upon the path between them: something which he would have liked to conceal, were it not plainly too late. His acute consciousness of this thing, his anxiety concerning it was beyond his control. Reflected in his demeanour, it reacted on Harland; who, after several polite attempts towards ignorance, felt his eyes drawn downwards to the spot on which the old man's disturbed attention was set. Then he saw at his feet a child's wooden horse: a bright, alluring creature in black and white paint, with scarlet leather reins. Elizabeth was justified. Plainly, the old chap was very queer.

There came to him the dim remembrance of some rare

form of insanity in which all the patient's mental habits are reversed.

He looked up, to find Farringdon's cold eyes fixed on him. They seemed to hold him in his place, to accuse him of trespass, of indecent curiosity, to demand some excuse or explanation. He had nothing to say; with him, an unusual circumstance. He told himself angrily that he was unaccustomed as yet to the society of harmless lunatics.

Then Farringdon said suddenly, "Found me out, eh?" It was a relief to hear his usual clipped and disagreeable accents. Harland, remembering the strange caressing voice which had greeted him as he came down the garden, said to himself that the paroxysm seemed to have passed.

He answered, "Hope I didn't startle you, sir. Careless of me to burst in on you like this. Elizabeth told me you were here: so I thought I would come and find you for myself." Not bad, he thought, for an amateur coming on these things unprepared. It was obviously the right line to take.

Farringdon looked at him contemptuously; then glanced at the horse, and said "You both think that I am going mad. Very natural."

Harland denied it: badly, nervously, in haste.

"Young men," said Farringdon in his nastiest tone, "like to confuse the incomprehensible and the insane."

Harland answered weakly, "Shouldn't think of it, sir! Shouldn't dream of interfering. I did not mean to intrude—sorry. Your private affairs—not my business."

"I am glad you realize that," said Farringdon: and again he glanced at the incriminating horse. Harland knew that it was, for both of them, the focal point of the strange picture in which they stood. Farringdon, though he might not be sane, fully realised the queerness of it; but he would give no explanation. Harland must pretend to ignore what he could not forget; as the civilised guest ignores some domestic privacy that meets his eye. What could the old beggar have been doing with it? A toy horse! The question throbbed in his brain. Entertaining some child? But there was no child: then—Farringdon and children! One couldn't connect them. He turned from the thing deliberately, and looked about him.

It was then that he perceived how great a change had been worked in the bit of trellised garden. He had stepped from the desert to the sown. The old brick wall had been cleansed of its smuttiness, and now shone rosy against the lucent winter sky. The little walk was newly gravelled. On each side the freshly raked beds seemed the warm homes of slumbrous living things. The winter had been a mild one: and already their soft blackness was marked, here and there, with pricking darts of green—the exhilarating upward pressure of new life. It all seemed extraordinarily inappropriate to the harsh-featured and colourless old man who stood on the clean bright gravel with a toy horse at his feet: yet his were the hands that had brought it about. He was looking at Harland with renewed annoyance and suspicion. Plainly, he dreaded further discoveries, and wished that his visitor were gone. Presently, perceiving the survey to be at an end, he said sharply, "Notice anything?"

"Why, yes of course I do," said Harland eagerly. "A great change, I shouldn't have recognised the place. Extraordinary improvement—I congratulate you, sir! Makes a most delightful little garden, and uncommonly private."

Farringdon answered, "That was essential. I did my best."

"I could hardly have believed," said Harland, still looking about him, noticing all the little careful touches of neatness and refinement, and sedulously avoiding the horse.

"That so much could have been made of it. One hardly feels as if one were in London. It must have been a tremendous piece of work." His true amazement, of course, centered not in this secret garden, but in Farringdon: that he should have contrived so fair a thing.

"That all?" said Farringdon. Harland thought that he detected a new note in his voice, as of a biting anxiety almost beyond his control. Was the old chap going to spring a further surprise on him?

"Of course," he said. "It's all very nice—charming. Wonderful lot you have got out of the space. It will be quite a picture when the bulbs are out."

Farringdon insisted, "You don't notice anything else?" He seemed determined to extort some admission.

Harland was confused, troubled. He suspected that the queerness was coming on again.

"No—no," he said. "I think not—nothing else."

"Poor fool!" said Farringdon.

Evidently the strained attention which had been demanded of Harland since he came to the end of the garden was beginning to tell on his nerves: for as Farringdon spoke, that cool and controlled attention broke suddenly. At those words of contemptuous pity, his consciousness slipped from the clutches of the problem which had been evoked by this horrid little scene, and was abruptly possessed by the all-absorbing memory of the woman whom he loved. The very fragrance of her personality was all about him. He had been on his way to visit her. Now, it seemed as though her spirit came to meet him. He was caught to a plane of consciousness where all who love are felt to be one. Through this sudden ecstasy of communion, this enraptured sense of a complete attainment, he heard, as it were, the echo of Farringdon's anxious and unlovely accents.

"You don't notice anything else?"

He didn't, of course. He was a man in love. His passions played strange tricks with him. Often in the night-time they had brought Ursula's image before his consciousness: in moments of silence and relaxation, had spoken to him with her voice.

Yet Farringdon's question persisted with him. Surely he did notice something—something besides that radiant personal vision which was so easily explicable in terms of common sense? Some new atmosphere, some vague yet powerful influence was in the place. It belonged, this "something," to Ursula: she stood for it, was in it. All the graciousness, the tender and sacred aspects of human intercourse seemed to be suggested to him; to make their presence felt, to call for his response. The confidence and companionship of woman and of man, all the holy bonds of mutual service and protection—he had never known their meaning till this hour. The unfolding and fresh blossoming of life, Childhood and Motherhood, the secret loveliness, the very magic of existence—they were all here, enfolding him as it were with wings of power, a ministering force. He gave himself to an exquisite dream, heard with the inward ear the eternal symphony of love and life, the soft movements of women, the joyous cries of little children. He forgot Farringdon; seeing as it were his own life unrolled before him, a thing of great nobility, a part of the very process of creation, filled with endless opportunities of self-giving love. The presence of Ursula persisted; the gathering-point of his consciousness, his link with his vital world. Gradually, holding as it were her spirit to his side, he withdrew from it, slid back, no longer alone, to his normal universe; and then perceived, as he had done an instant before, that of course there was nothing there—only the neat and sheltered little garden, dreary in the gathering dusk, and old Farringdon, who was now looking at him curiously; studying him, as one might study a case.

In a moment of time they seemed to have changed places. Harland, who had no love for the things of the imagination, felt like an ass. He was convinced that his face had betrayed that brief and silent ecstasy: no doubt in some silly way, by flushed cheeks or widened eyes. He knew exactly what had happened: Farringdon's queer, disturbing behaviour and his own seething emotions had produced something which nearly approached hallucination, but could probably be explained in physiological terms. He was filled with disgust: and seized, meanly enough, on the first weapon of defence that came to hand.

He glanced at the toy horse, and said firmly, "Look here, Sir, you're not well. I'm certain you're not. Better have some advice."

Farringdon answered, "I am getting well. It has been a long illness; but now I am being cured."

The answer baffled Harland, whose one longing was for instant escape. He said to himself that he would think things over quietly, and come again. Farringdon's ironic smile followed him down the square, assuring him that his foolish moment of obsession had been known and understood; that henceforth they were partners in "queerness." "Young men like to confuse the incomprehensible and the insane." Harland's experience, of course, was comprehensible enough: yet somehow he had lost all taste for judgments of this kind. They seemed dangerous. In spite of his brave words, he knew that now he could never betray Farringdon's mania; never procure for him that threatened "advice." They shared a secret, shared a garden. His deeper mind was sure of it, despite the protesting voice of common sense.

He came to Ursula still pursued by that elusive vision. It possessed him, gave him courage; promising an added glory to existence giving great meanings to all outward things. Her presence renewed its magic, seemed a part of it. He asked her to be his wife.

Their engagement was three or four weeks old when he first spoke to her of Farringdon. His inner life was now calm and appeased; his days full of an eager expectancy, a busy planning of all the outward circumstances that belonged to the making of their home. The incidents of that troubled afternoon, those queer moments at the end of the garden, were dim. True, he had been filled for an instant with strange sensations: but they were natural to an emotional crisis. A man is not normal at such a time: his nerves betray him. Some deep insistent voice whispered to him that he was reading events backwards; that the emotional crisis had resulted from the events of the afternoon.

But he disliked this voice—he called it fancy—and refused to hear it. Only in one direction did he permit its influence. It made him extremely unwilling to revisit old Farringdon. He secretly dreaded the little sheltered garden, and the new intimacy that was between them. Inadvertently, they had penetrated each other's defences. Some part of his being, deep buried beneath the crust of educated common sense, knew Farringdon's secret. He hated to think of the moment in which that knowledge should reach his surface-mind, and become his secret too.

Meanwhile there was the old man, living alone: getting, perhaps, queerer. It was very well to put matters on an imaginative basis: but the toy horse remained unexplained—inexplicable. Harland knew that he could not drop the thing, wipe it from his memory, as he wished. He must go back sooner or later, must look after Farringdon. The prospect was horrible. The dreary note of stagnation and lovelessness, the old man's drab and chilly demeanour—his lifted nostril, cold eyes, contemptuous smile—all these were inimical to Harland's mood, seemed an insult to his eager crescent manhood, his victorious love. He would have to mention his engagement. He resented in advance the curt sarcastic comments it was likely to call forth. Even the criticisms of a lunatic are detestable when one is in love.

But he went. In an expansive moment he told Ursula of Farringdon; of his queer, inhuman life, repellant ways, his threatened insanity—he called it that. Her interest and compassion shamed and moved him. She said, "Poor, poor old man! All those years wasted! Suffering, perhaps knowing he was wretched and lonely all the time. And now there's no one to help him to love—and of course he can't do it all alone. And that garden—petting his bulbs, because he has nothing else that's alive—"

Harland said in self-defence there was more behind it than that: he fancied the old man had delusions. He mentioned the horse.

Ursula exclaimed "*Delusions?* how *can* you be so dense? It's heart-breaking! Don't you see—don't you feel—it's all part of it? He's been trying to make believe there's a child because he was something alive and soft and growing, that he can help. He's waking up—trying at the last minute to conjure up the life that he's missed. And he can't get it, poor old thing, and you don't help him; when it's all been so easy for us!"

"Why do you think that?" asked Harland meekly.

She was full of these imaginative charities, ever ready

for a soul hunt. Her generous thoughts soon crystallized to facts. Still, he remembered hearing Farringdon's happy and caressing voice when he was alone at the end of the garden; and with less equanimity, certain incidents of his own swift experience. Certainly these things were compatible with Ursula's absurd theory.

She looked at him now with wet eyes, and answered, "I know it—I feel it. It *can't* be anything else."

"He's pretty disagreeable still, anyhow," said Harland.

"Shy," said Ursula.

Of course in the end she sent him to Farringdon: sent him with strict injunctions to show friendliness, to break down defences, prepare the way for her own visit. She was fired by her theory, full of it: plainly intended to associate herself with his tardy salvation. The missionary spirit burned bright in her. Her love seemed to pass through Harland, gathering ardour on its way, and pour itself out, eager and merciful, upon all the world. It infected him: so that he actually went, at last, with a determination to accomplish something—to be useful to old Farringdon if he could.

But he did not intend to risk the strange magic of that garden. It was only self-suggestion, of course: still, these experiences are disturbing and unpleasant. So he was ready for Elizabeth when she opened the door, and said promptly, "I've come to see Mr. Farringdon. If he is in the garden, you might tell him that I am here."

He went into the study: and thence saw Elizabeth's reluctant figure going down the garden path. When she was near the trellis she stopped, and called loudly, "Mr. Farringdon! Mr. Harland is here." It was curious behaviour in a well-trained servant: but Farringdon, who appeared immediately, did not seem to be annoyed. Perhaps she was obeying orders. He came stiffly up the path with his neat little footsteps; and Harland, watching him. detected for the first time in his movements the on-coming feebleness and difficulty of age. He entered by the study window, and said, "Ah, Harland. I expected you before this. Was afraid you were going to be a nuisance. Come to see whether I am getting worse?"

"I just looked in," said Harland swiftly, "to have a little chat. Ought to have come long ago! So many things to do—time passes! Fact is, I have some news for you. I am going to be married."

"Ah!" said Farringdon. "Ah!" His expression changed. Suspicion left it. He pondered. Presently he observed, "That explains it. No doubt you are in love."

Harland resented the suggestion. This was worse than he had expected. He told himself he was damned if he would give himself away to the old curmudgeon: provoke his sneers about sentiment and so on. One's feelings were one's own!

Then he remembered Ursula's orders: her enthusiastic certainties, her generosity, her faith. His feelings were his own no more.

"You saw them," said Farringdon, still pondering, "that day at the end of the garden. No not *saw*, perhaps: that is too much. But you felt their presence—you knew."

"I was—well—afraid I may have behaved a bit oddly—perhaps I wasn't quite myself that day," said Harland. "Curious! No accounting for these sensations."

Farringdon replied, "For a moment you were your real self."

His words brought back a vivid memory of that strange and glorious instant of illusion.

He went on in a new and almost conciliatory tone. "I wonder how much you understood?"

Harland said "I—oh well—there was nothing definite, nothing one could lay hold of, you know. Odd—very! Just an impression, a passing feeling. Suggestion, no doubt."

"Ah yes!" said Farringdon, the old snarl in his voice again. "Suggestion, no doubt! You young men are so clever. Any psychological claptrap is better than the truth."

Harland was determined to be patient. "You see, sir," he said, "I'm quite in the dark; and you, apparently, have the explanation. I am bound to confess that one felt a curious atmosphere; emotional, and so on. That was really all."

"One felt," said Farringdon abruptly, "'the atmosphere and influence of women and little children—homeliness and love—wasn't that it?"

Harland had to agree. That was it. Then he remembered Ursula's explanation of the horse. It all fitted in. Obviously, the old man's delusions took this form. He forgot that he had shared them.

"I am glad that you felt it too," said Farringdon slowly. "At first I was anxious that the secret should be kept. One disliked, naturally enough, the imputation of insanity, and that was bound to come. No one would believe in anything so beautiful and true. But it is right that others should know their generosity and pity; how life breaks through, how—one is saved."

Generosity and pity—that, for Harland, linked the unknown with Ursula again: with her self-giving compassion for all sad and lonely creatures. The thing grew more amazing. One could not connect Farringdon with theories of redemption, theological or other: still less with a gratitude which overpowered a lifetime of suspicion and reserve. Harland was moved by it—by the spectacle of this gnarled and lonely human creature struggling to make a breach in the wall that hemmed him in. Those words, *How one is saved*, melted him; for had not Ursula saved his life from unreality?

His inarticulate sympathy made a bridge between them; so that something in Farringdon's fortifications suddenly fell away. He began to speak; harshly, gruffly, yet with an overpowering simplicity and eagerness. "You young men," he said, "so busy living, you don't realize what it is to find out that one is old, very old, come to the end; and that one has never lived, never broken through. You are living now—you have got out of your shell—you are saved from it. But I could not break through. My body was against me. Some are, even from the first, harsh, hard, shy, difficult! When I was young, I loved no one. Afraid to. Always defended myself. So it set in the wrong shape; hemmed me in. Now, it will never be able to express a soul. Listen to my voice—attractive, isn't it? Beats people off: and I'm locked up inside. To wake up alive—know that you're there—catch glimpses—and never to get out—that's hell."

Harland could not reply. He had caught for an instant a glimpse of the famished spirit behind its barriers: and realised with shame that for years he had visited the hungry and had never given it bread.

Then the unattractive voice spoke again: words inappropriate to their speaker. "But some," it said, "get a second chance. Spirit to spirit—wonderful. No veil between—"

It is a strange experience when the anguished and stifled heart of one whom we have long classified as heartless suddenly speaks. Harland, listening to Farringdon's terse, reluctant statements, felt like a person who hears some spiritual melody, full of the magic of the infinite, ground out by a harsh and ill-constructed gramophone. In spite of the creaking machinery, his inward ear detected the celestial harmony. It was still the old icy manner, the hard inhuman tone—the words tossed at him, unwillingly, as from a mind that shunned all contact with men. But that hard inhuman tone was telling superhuman secrets: saying that its owner—the close-veiled smothered unattractive soul of Farringdon—had spoken spirit to spirit, wonderful; no veil between!

Harland did not know that his own spirit, the immortal humanity of him which had awakened to life at Ursula's touch, was now looking out at old Farringdon through his eyes: but Farringdon saw it, and responded to its silent questions. The intimacy between them was now complete.

"It began," he said, "because I wanted it. Never had let myself want anything outside myself before. Thought it foolish—dangerous, too. But shut up here waiting for death, nothing else—this solitude—this narrow awful life—it grew and grew till it broke me at last. Ghastly; unendurable! Couldn't make friends now—contacts with men and women. Shut off too long—bearish—old—shy—hopeless! Had to be helped—couldn't ask, explain: and you young people—too busy. Natural enough."

Harland again felt extremely ashamed of himself.

"But *they* helped," said Farringdon. His grating voice took a hushed note, as if he spoke of sacred things. "*They* came. Pitied one! I wanted something—didn't know what—craved for it—and they came. It seemed to open a door, and they came in. The spirits of the women and the children! Happy, friendly. All one had missed. Parsons used to say, 'Ask and ye shall receive'—probably say it still. Mere words; they don't know. And you young fellows have got your explanation—eh? Some damned psychological rot."

The normal Farringdon appeared for an instant upon the surface: and Harland said eagerly, "Quite! quite!" Here were at least two words that he could understand.

"Simple enough!" said Farringdon musingly. "You stretch out—beyond yourself—and something meets you. There are the facts. Same in ordinary life—love, and so on—I suppose?"

"Quite! Quite!" said Harland again. He felt shy.

Farringdon went on. "People must wonder, when they lose them— Accidents, bereavements, why they go, are caught away. When they came to me, I saw the horror of it: the torture and loneliness, how they must be missed." The hoarse old voice shook, as if Farringdon the self-sufficient and exclusive were actually grieving for all the unknown sorrow of the world. "Babies—born for death! Germs of unused life. Little soft gay growing things cut off. Women, full of unspent tenderness, caught away: torn from the plait of life. It must seem hard to understand. But all there, if we'll call upon them. All wanting to give their love, to make a link. That's their destiny—that's what they go for. None of it lost. Another chance for us: for the old, poor fools who have missed it—haven't lived."

So *that* was it.

"But it's hard," said Farringdon, "to find things that one can give, can do for them: to work for them; as of course one must. Down there at the end of the garden—that's our home. They come to me when they can. There's a door there, you know—an old door. I'd never used it. And doors open on other worlds than those we see. That's another thing I found out. Shut doors shut out everything. They came to me through that door. It made a way for them—my opening it. Been shut for years. When the loneliness broke me, I unlocked it; and they came in. I did my best: tried toys for the little ones. You saw that horse last time you came. Naturally enough, it convinced you that I was insane. I'd forgotten to throw it away. It was no use. They can't get at toys—all shadowy to them—not real—not alive. Flowers are different. Those are really alive, you see: and so they are the same for them as for us.

"So that seemed all that I could do: to make their garden beautiful for them when they came. I work away at it, and hope to please them. It is not much. Still, it makes a home; shows that one cares. And *they* miss the home life, too—"

Harland was lost. It was all so actual and convincing: and so absurd. That old Farringdon should commune with the spirits of the dead at the end of a London garden. Why not here, in the house? or anywhere? why not—? He stopped, realizing that such questions were almost a confession of faith.

Farringdon stood up.

"Do you care," he said, "to come down to the garden?" The tone was of one conferring great honour on his guest.

They went down the path: Harland, as he expressed it, keeping a firm hold on himself, Farringdon plainly absorbed in the magic of his dream. He passed round the trellis and said, "Yes, I have come back," as if in answer to a question unheard. Then he turned back to Harland and said, "You see, here they are. They wait for me," and went forward to the wicker seat which had been placed at the further end.

For a moment Harland saw the empty, clean and exquisitely kept bit of garden, the neat beds, now green and tufted with the upstanding leaves and swelling buds of early daffodils; and the old man, victim of pathetic illusions, sitting there alone with an eager unsuitable smile on his hard mouth. Then, suddenly, the place was full of unaccountable life. It came not from some far-off, transcendent sphere of existence, but was there, all about them, actual and insistent: poured out, as it were, from its own inwardness. They were caught in the meshes of it: in the texture of a real, existent world abruptly disclosed. He heard in the deepening outward silence the gay cries of little unseen children that raced upon the paths: felt one who brushed past him, just escaping a fall. A tiny hand, he fancied, was at the dangling charm of his watch chain. Just for an instant the soft down upon some little head nestled warm against his hand. He had forgotten the use of eyes and ears: and had slipped to a plane of consciousness beyond their explorations, where he knew that which his senses could not perceive. The women were there too: gentle, pitiful women; strong-souled, generous mothers; young, eager women, early cut off from human love and work. They clustered about the poor, trapped soul of Farringdon. They were helping him, tearing down the barriers that shut him from real life, feeding his starved and sterile heart. Harland the practical, the well-conducted, the prosaic, saw, in a great vision, this angelic ministry pressing in, everywhere, upon reluctant humanity; spending upon the living the treasures of its love. He even divined how many such eager hands had made the way plain between himself and Ursula, how many presences had blessed the lighting of the flame of their joint lives.

And thinking of her, as before, concrete reality rolled back on him abruptly. He was in the empty garden: and Farringdon sat upon the wicker seat alone. It had all gone beyond his reach. He could not find it. But the old man, as he saw, was still in the presence of his friends. Safely fenced in by those unseen verities, that ring of ministering love, he had forgotten Harland and showed no sign of interest when he went silently away.

Of course Ursula got the truth from him, even so far as he was able to tell it. He was amazed to find how quietly she took this incredible extension of their world. Chiefly she was glad for old Farringdon, with the unselfish delight of a missionary who observes his fellow labourer's success.

"He doesn't," she said, "want us any more really: that's quite clear. He's all right with them. It's glorious. I thought when you told me about him first, that we might have helped him. Showed him the way out. Made friends. But it's out of our hands altogether. He'll never make links on our side now. It's because, you know, he's so old. He's standing at the very edge—and when he opened that door, he looked through."

"How do you know?" said Harland: the helpless question of adoring common sense confronted by intuitive sympathy.

"I saw it somehow when you were telling me," said Ursula. "And that, you see, is why he felt he *must* plant flowers. They've been growing with him bit by bit: coming out of the earth to the light. Presently they will blossom. And he will too. He's like one of those great buds, growing and breaking out from its dry brown sheath. It's his first spring."

She spoke with authority: seemed to be looking at a celestial garden, where the growing upwards of Farringdon's soul from the hard and crusted winter earth was helped by small and gentle hands. Presently she added thoughtfully, "But I expect the flowering will be on the other side."

A few weeks afterwards, he took her to pay the long-promised visit to old Farringdon. It was a March day, fine, with a gentle wind; full of the soft, exciting messages of coming life. As they climbed the square they saw in gardens that looked southward the first golden blooms unfurling to the sun. Harland said, "I'm glad we waited till today. It seems appropriate. The old chap's daffodils will be in flower."

Elizabeth opened the door. Her expression was more

than ordinarily harassed. Mr. Farringdon, she said, had been down in the garden all day; hadn't been in to lunch. Yes, she called him as usual but he had given special orders that he was not to be disturbed. Unusually queer he'd been lately. Dreamy-like. She didn't like to see it. One thing, he seemed happy enough, always pottering over his precious flowers. But he had lost his old sharp manner; and she thought it a bad sign.

Harland said, "We'll go and find him"; and Ursula added suddenly, "If he is still there."

They went down the garden path in silence, the heavenly blue and white above them, the scampering clouds and approached with their insistent vitality its sterile grime. Harland called, "Mr. Farringdon, are you there? I have brought Ursula to see you." But there was no reply.

After a moment, he left her and went round the trellis alone. The little garden was in perfect order. It seemed to him that a great peace brooded upon it: a sense of life and loveliness achieved. The early daffodils were all in bloom: clean, radiant, erect. The soft black beds shone with their triumphant vindication of beauty distilled, forced into freedom, from the common stuff of earth. Old Farringdon lay amongst his flowers: surrounded on all sides by those antique and exquisite symbols of Life eternally renewed. His body was dead. Harland observed without surprise that the garden gate was open.

* * *

Outro: Provenance

The other six stories in this collection and all of the poems were published by Underhill during her lifetime. This story—the longest of the bunch—remained a typed manuscript in the King's College London archives in London for decades before its first publication in this book.

The manuscript itself is a layered bit of archaeology. There is a typewritten original version that has no date. Then there are corrections—some in pen and some in pencil—that appear to have been made over the course of several revisions. It is plausible that the original composition date of "At the End of the Garden" matched the other six stories in this collection and that it remained unpublished for one reason or another. It is possible that this story would have appeared in *Horlick's* had the magazine not ceased publication in 1905. There is no way to tell given what remains in her archives. What is certain, however, is that it is the result of at least three phases of composition, as indicated by the layers of revision apparent on the manuscript itself. The changes she made were not heavy revisions. Often, she made modifications for clarity or to add imagery to a particular phrase. There are few substantial revisions and none that affect anything particularly significant.

Independent of our speculation about the provenance of this story, it is clear that this one stands out among the rest for several thematic reasons. Yes, there is the central character, a haunted, male character who is experiencing the mystical as a numinous feminine presence, a motif that makes this story similar to others in this collection. Yet there is a missing intensity in the experience of the supernatural in this particular story that makes it feel to us as if it were the work of a younger Underhill, one influenced by the Gothic tradition that includes the ghosts of children and hidden doors to other worlds. By the time she was writing "The Mountain Image" and "Ivory Tower," her depictions of the mystical experience had become deeply other-worldly. In

"At the End of the Garden" the ghosts remain children as children always have been while their mothers care for them as any terrestrial mother would. Their presence is soothing to old Farringdon; there is nothing dangerous about them at all. It makes the most sense that this story is an early effort by Underhill, one she considered saving—witness the revisions—but ultimately abandoned.

Of course, this is all speculation. Not nearly enough survives of Underhill's notebooks and drafts to make any sort of definitive assessment. We have placed the story here, in the middle of our collection, to hedge our bets a bit.

FOR HILDA

(*Theophanies* v–vi)

Sweet fennel in our garden grows,
White lavender, and herb of grace.
Cat-mint and thyme its edges close;
It is a green and silver place
Where marjoram, basil, maudlein, cicely
Make scented melody.

There rosemary and balm are found
Wherewith the wounds of life are healed;
There humble woodruff mats the ground
And hoards the magic of the field.
The holy vervein, hyssop, bergamot
Give blessing to the plot.

Those hasty hearts that hurry by
the coloured borders to applaud
Know not the hidden worlds that lie
Within these narrow coffers stored;
Yet, to the gentle touch of those who seek,
the herbs in fragrance speak.

Then in the prudent mind's defence
Of welded thought, a breach is made
And down the alley-ways of sense
Strange poignant dreams of soul invade—
News from beyond our stubborn ramparts blown,
and here in perfume known.

Those ramparts, they are builded tall;
But we a secret gate possess
That opens in the outer wall
What time its living latch we press:
A little emerald gate, that sets us free
Within eternity.

* * *

Outro: News from Beyond

We spoke about the unknown date of composition for the story "At the End of the Garden" and ended up speculating that the story was likely the effort of a very young Underhill, one whose fiction-writing chops matured by the time she published her five stories in 1904-5. This poem might complicate that guess. Here is another garden that is filled with species native to the United Kingdom, any of which would be welcome in a London garden. As in the preceding story, this garden, too, has a doorway that leads to "hidden worlds." The poem was published in the collection *Theophanies* in 1916, although there is no way to know the date of its original composition. It came first in the collection and, as it title indicates, acts as the dedication for the book.

The theophany here is the fragrance of the garden's flowers in bloom. Their many and intense scents bring "news from beyond" as well as "strange poignant dreams."

OUR LADY OF THE GATE

IT WAS IN the hour before Matins, and the night was very dark. The Convent of S. Paolo-al-Monte slept, like the tired earth; only the Father Porter stood at the gate, and looked out to where he knew the hills lay, on the opposite side of the valley. It was a fancy of his so to seek the fringe of the cloister, and breathe the air that came up from the great world whilst the rest of the brotherhood slept.

From where he stood, a steep pathway dropped to the high road which ran along the river-valley on its way from Perugia to Rome; and a descending line of roofs beside it marked the stations of the Way of the Cross with their shrines. The Father Porter had sometimes thought in the daytime that the low cry of sacramental pain came up to him from those places—that so actual a symbolism must bring with it a real Victim to the sacrifice, so that the offering of the ages was re-enacted on the Umbrian hill; for he was of a romantic disposition, and had been esteemed as a poet in the world. Now the emblems of atonement, too, rested from their work of intercession, and the convent wall threw its kindly shadow upon them.

The Father Porter's eyes wandered slowly down to the valley. He heard the river, whose voice is drowned of a morning by the washerwomen's chatter, talking softly to itself. He saw the road, a grey and misty streak, running friendlily beside it; and thought, with a pleasant but unauthorised melancholy, of the wonderful cities full of aesthetic excitements towards which it ran. The road was to him a symbol of many things which he had denied himself, but could not quite forget. As he watched, his fancies ran along it, as electricity runs along the easiest path.

So watching, he presently became conscious that something besides his own dream was travelling that night. He saw a moving shadow on the road. The Father Porter congratulated himself piously on his good fortune. In Umbria, as a rule, one does not walk of a night time; and many vigils might have been kept at the gateway without yielding such an incident as this. The shadow, he saw, was approaching the hill of the convent: presently it would pass beneath him, near but unknowable, and fade along the way that led to Rome. There was a completeness in the prospect which appealed to his artistic sense; and he watched the traveller very intently, speculating idly as to whom it might be. Indistinctly seen in the darkness, one apprehended a cloaked figure, vague of outline—something, he thought, like the Mater Dolorosa, who shared the agony of her Son in the shrines upon the Pilgrim's Way.

But at the foot of the hill the shadow seemed to linger, and the watcher's attention became more earthly, more alert. He peered into the darkness, focussing his stare; and whilst he peered, it vanished entirely from his sight.

Then the Father Porter so far forgot the dignity of his office as to go a step or two beyond the gate; for he was roused from his usual calm. Long custom told him that this could have only one meaning—the traveller was coming up the Pilgrim's Way towards the convent gate. He had watched many so come; had seen them turn the corner by the image of Christ before Pilate, and presently reappear upon the stony slope. But orthodox pilgrims, in his experience, did not come singly and by night, and the community knew no other visitors. So now he waited and strained his eyes, rather breathless and excited. When one watches the world from a lonely hill-top, the mind reacts quickly to small stimuli from without. He hoped the bell would not call him to Matins before this little adventure came to an end.

The time, as he waited, seemed to pass very slowly. He was alone with his own curiosity, which was half eager and half fearful, in a darkness through which, he knew, a stranger approached him. After the first moment of surprise, the sensation was more disagreeable than romantic. Knowing every step of the path, he could calculate to an instant how long one should take between the first shrine and the last; and it seemed to him that this traveller took far longer than he had any reason to expect. At last he began to wonder in his impatience whether the shadow had been anything more than an illusion of sense. It came into his mind that perhaps it was a device of the Enemy to tempt him from pious meditation. He recited a Paternoster with great devotion.

At the last words he looked up, and fear was replaced by certainty. The mysterious visitor stood before him.

It was a woman—a woman alone, by night at the gate of a Franciscan house. The thrill of worldly excitement which the Father Porter had felt gave way to a panic of modesty. He had desired adventures, a thing unbecoming to the demure emotions of the cloister; and Heaven had administered condign punishment. Contrition, no less than decorum, kept his eyes fixed on the ground and his hands discreetly hidden in the folds of his large sleeves; whilst visions of probable complications and inevitable explanations drove the poetry of the situation from his mind.

Meanwhile the woman stood quietly before him. She was tall and upright; a long shawl, flung over her head, wrapped her round, and gave to her that shrouded look which had first caught the Father Porter's eye. The blackness of the night helped a certain ghostliness of outline. For some minutes, the two faced one another in silence which gathered weight from the darkness and the hour, till the strain began to tell upon the Father Porter's always sensitive and now much shaken nerves. With an ear anxiously attentive for the sound of the Matins bell, which he knew to be imminent, his mind was searching hastily for any means of escape from this shockingly irregular interview.

At last, "What would you, my sister?" he said, in a small and timid voice.

"I have come on a visit to the convent," said the woman; and there was a decided ring of firmness and authority in her tone which made the Father Porter look up with some suddenness. He was a short, stout person, and the stranger towered over him by several inches.

A curious sinking sensation came over him then; for it seemed to him that he was looking into a worn but beautiful face, very dim and white against the folds of the shawl, and that eyes of a marvellous blue met his and smiled gravely. She wore a little wooden cross suspended from a string at her throat—altogether a strange apparition to meet on an Umbrian hill-top before the dawn. The novelty and mystery of the thing, acting on a mind that leaned naturally towards the fanciful and the occult, were upsetting the Father Porter a little. The adventurous mind can survive the religious habit; and to the mind that waits on adventure, adventure is sure to come. He lost sight abruptly of the unlawfulness of his position, and the obligations of his office, and swung back to that country of legend which never lies very far from convent gates.

Old histories of Holy Appearances rose up before him. He felt a sudden and inexplicable conviction that this could be no ordinary pilgrim in search of a cheap indulgence; and an unreasoning awe fell upon his spirit. With the awe his faith was strengthened; for reverence always crushes incredulity. It seemed quite clear that he, and his convent through him, were about to be the recipients of some signal grace. He thought of San Bernardo, and other entertainers of the Blest, and tried vainly to decide what behaviour was best suited to the emergency; for time pressed, and already he fancied that he could hear the footsteps of the community on their way to chapel. But no holy ejaculations came to his trembling lips, and he was obliged to fall back on the ordinary phrases of human intercourse.

He pulled himself together with an effort.

"What is your business with the brotherhood, my sister?" he said.

"I have come upon my son's business," answered the visitor. Again the Father Porter noticed a heightened dignity in her tone; and a thrill of pious fear passed through him as he realised the mystical significance of her words.

She gave him no time for further consideration, but added immediately:—

"I have come a long way. I am very weary. Is there no place for pilgrims in the convent?"

The Father stood aside hastily; and now it seemed to him that her mantle was of deepest blue, like the sky behind her, and that a faint light shone from her little cross. The swift poetry of the Italian night had him in its grasp, and drove out the last remnants of worldly reason: and an overwrought imagination, long denied adequate nourishment, gave itself up incontinently to the promptings of pious romance.

"It is the Blessed Madonna herself!" he muttered; and the first stroke of the Matins bell, very clear and low, came with its reminder of heavenly mysteries to vanquish his last hesitating doubts.

"Enter, Holy Mother," he cried; and, in the same breath, as he fell on his knees, "*Ave Maria gratia plena.*"

The woman said nothing more, but passed by him through the gate, and so into the outer courtyard. Opposite the gate, the doors of the chapel stood open, and a faint light came through them from where the novices with their torches waited for the lector to begin. The bell had ceased. The Father Porter, for the first time within his recollection, was late for the Office.

Discipline demanded that he should immediately hurry towards the choir, but this was no moment for such thoughts. Respect for the Heavenly Visitor and obedience to the Rule struggled fiercely together in his breast. Even in his present exalted state, he knew that his position was difficult. Should he keep the marvellous tidings secret, and presently see the Holy One discovered, and driven out even as an earthly woman, to the convent's undying disgrace? Or should he go to the Father Superior, and discover to him the favour that had been manifested to the community? Now the Father Superior was old, dim-sighted, and rather deaf, but remnants of the shrewd common sense which had distinguished him in his prime were still occasionally noticeable. He loved the straight high-roads of religion, and still kept an acid tongue and a fund of dialectic for the summary discouragement of mysticism. Moreover, at Matins he was always cold and sleepy, and did not abound in the sweet reasonableness of the saints. The Father Porter felt that the moment was scarcely propitious for transcendental revelations.

But as he pondered and stumbled over the dilemma of instant choice, and tried in vain to hold fast by the mood of tranquil ecstasy in which he felt that his master, St. Francis, would have welcomed such a Presence at his gates, he saw the visitor slowly cross the courtyard and pass through the chapel doors. It seemed to him then that her feet did not move upon the pavement, and that other and sweeter music mingled with the *Venite* which the brothers were beginning to chant. She entered the chapel, and he was alone in the dark. A sudden terror of solitude descended on him, and he crept after her with uncertain footsteps, feeling peculiarly human and afraid.

She had paused in front of the Chapel of Rest, where a red lamp burned before the Host, and now she knelt at the first step of its altar in prayer. He remembered her words, "I have come on my Son's business," and made his obeisance and passed on in breathless awe lest he should intrude upon that Sacramental Converse. And so, coming to the choir, it seemed the most natural thing in the world that he should slip into his stall next to that of the Father Cellarer, and join his weak and shaky voice to the cry of "*Sicut erat in principio*" with the remainder of the brotherhood.

It was Sunday morning. As the Psalms and lessons followed each other in due order the Father Porter's spiritual exaltation increased.

"*Probasti cor meum et visitasti nocte*," he sang, and the solemn magic of the Liturgy wrapped him round, and clothed his secret thoughts in a language of praise. Heavenly roses and lilies, he knew, were lending their perfume to the incense; the knowledge of a Divine Presence became every instant more real. He was living again the Contemplative Life, after many years of placid stagnation. A subtle shame for hours spent in the pursuit of sensuous images and perfect phrases came over him; he remembered with loathing certain sonnets in the manner of Petrarca, which, though written in the hours set apart for meditation, were scarcely Franciscan in tone. Old ideals crept back, he recaptured the essence of youthful devotion. He knew now that he was bound to tell the brotherhood of the wonder that had been shown to him that night. The heavenly news had eclipsed the earthly inconvenience.

The tall, quiet figure still knelt before the Chapel of Rest; and still the brethren, their eyes bent down devoutly, sung on and saw her not. So Matins were finished, and after them Lauds, and the community rose and filed slowly out of the choir. Each one as he passed by the place where the Blessed Sacrament lay, turned and made a deep obeisance. It pleased the Father Porter to think that More than they knew was there to receive their homage. They went back to the cloister with heads bowed meekly down, and their folded hands discreetly covered by the sleeve, as the Rule demands. They had noticed nothing.

Only the first and last of the procession, the Father Superior, whose blindness was of a partial nature and did not extend to such things as it was desirable that he should not perceive; and the youngest of the novices, a fresh country boy from the valleys below Perugia, had seen perhaps more than the rest. The youngest of the novices had not yet learnt that humility walks with eyes modestly downcast. The Father Superior knew watchfulness to be a duty of his office. So eager youth and meticulous age both went out filled with a very great surprise; but whilst the novice's eyes were bright and his lips smiling, the corners of the Father Superior's eye-brows were lifted up in a very forbidding way, and his lips looked thinner than usual. And when the community was ranged in order along the side of the cloister, the Father Porter was sent for, and asked, with considerable terseness, to explain the meaning of a woman's presence inside the gates.

It was still very dark and ghostly in the cloister, and once away from the comforting environment created by incense and psalm, the Father Porter became his earthly self again. He felt absurdly nervous for the recipient of a Divine Manifestation, and his breath, coming quickly in the stillness of the night, smote rather irritatingly upon the Father Superior's ear, and caused him to sniff in a very discouraging manner. All the ardours of the mystic and the poet were surging in the Father Porter's heart, but the chill of his surroundings made adequate speech difficult. So he began rather lamely at first, and told in unimpressive mutterings how Madonna had come to him at the gateway, with a cross that shone on her breast and a strange light on her face, and had demanded admittance in the name of her Son.

So told, in the presence of the actual and comfortable brothers, with the familiar staircase leading to the dormitory near at hand, it all seemed very improbable and fantastic. The Father Superior did not conceal his disgust.

But as he told, the magic of the vision came back to

the Father Porter. He was not a poet for nothing, and those trembling raptures of the spirit which had awoke in him to greet her, overflowed into his words. So that the brothers who stood round crept closer, and caught something of his emotion; and he stopped at last in the midst of a hushed silence.

And no one noticed that the youngest of the novices had gone quietly away whilst he spoke.

Now the face of the Father Superior was like nothing so much as the moon's face on a night of windy clouds; for disgust had made way for amazement, and amazement for uneasy belief, before the Father Porter had finished his tale. The thing, he knew, was incredible; and yet, supposing it were true? He was called upon to believe that such things had occasionally happened; and it would be a serious matter for the convent if he made a mistake, involving not only a spiritual, but also a financial loss. Pilgrims are profitable, and latter-day miracles rare. Still, there were disadvantages. He had, for instance, grave doubts as to this perfect efficiency as the host of a heavenly guest, for disuse had robbed his spiritual conversation of its early graces. For all these reasons, a very human sense of worry was mingled with his astonishment; but there was no uncertainty in his mind as to his immediate course of action.

In all proveable matters, test first and believe afterwards had been—even in theology—his invariable rule; so now he turned back towards the chapel, and the brothers trooped after him in all the ecstasy of holy inquisitiveness. Daylight was beginning to come, and a queer, grey radiance drew down from the window in the East. At the Chapel of Rest the Father Superior stayed his footsteps, and crossed himself with great devotion. The brethren did likewise, and then timidly raised their eyes. Some shaded their foreheads with one hand, as if they feared the Ineffable Glory. But all of them looked.

And what they saw was a tall, gaunt woman sitting on the altar steps. She was wrapped in a coarse shawl, her face was lined and wrinkled by many toils, and strands of grey hair lay on her forehead. But her eyes, which matched the Umbrian hills for blueness, were not dimmed, and on her face was the glory of great content. And at her feet sat the youngest of the novices, and as the brotherhood looked in silent horror on this sacrilege, he raised up his face to hers, and she bent slowly towards him, and they kissed one another. Then the Father Porter gave a great cry, for his spirit was much disturbed by what he saw; and the youngest of the novices, hearing that cry, turned quickly and saw all the community standing closely about him, and watching him with an astonished attention. He was only a boy, full of impulse and easily abashed; so that now he rose in great confusion, and came blushing very hotly to kneel at the Father Superior's feet.

His words gave great relief to the Father Superior, though the Father Porter found them very hard to bear.

"Oh reverend Father," he said, "will you not give us your blessing? It is my mother who has come up to see me."

*

But it is said that the Father Porter still makes his devotions to Our Lady, who came to him at the gate.

* * *

Outro: That Which Is Sought and Loved but Not Known and Possessed

There are three major influences on this story that demonstrate what Evelyn Underhill was studying in the first decade of the twentieth century.

The first is the work she did compiling the miracle stories and legends that surround the Virgin Mary for her *The Miracles of Our Lady Saint Mary* (1905). Underhill translated all kinds of stories from manuscripts in French and Latin and, in some cases, heavily edited them for her collection. She explains in her introduction:

> They are the fairy-tales of mediaeval Catholicism; the result of the reaction of religion on that spirit which produced the romances of chivalry. These tales bring us to the Courts of Paradise, but the atmosphere is still that of the Courts of Love. By turns homely and heroic, visionary and realistic, they do in literature that which the Gothic sculptors do in art; make a link between heaven and earth, give actual and familiar significance to the most awful mysteries of faith, and set the Queen of Angels in the midst of her faithful friends." (Underhill *Miracles* xiv)

Reading the tales she collected for her book, one sees instantly the power of the local legends of Mary and how she intervened in everyday life.

The second influence shown here relates to her travels throughout Europe with her mother, traveling to various churches and monasteries hidden all around Europe. She writes in her journal of her trip to the Umbrian hills in April 1902 most particularly, describing how life seems to be a mixture of the ancient and the modern, the holy and profane. She also writes of seeing the works of Pietro Perugino (1446–1523), and perhaps it is his *Pieta* that inspired the last scene between the young priest and his mother. Underhill's journals were collected posthumously by her good friend Lucy Menzies who edited and published them in 1949 with the title *Shrines and Cities of France and Italy*.

The third is the concept of the monastery or convent as she refers to the central place of the story. Medieval convents were mostly wiped out in England so would have been of great interest to Underhill in her desire to become a Roman Catholic. In *The Holy Rule of St. Benedict*, Rule 66 states that a porter shall have duties that match exactly the Father Porter in Underhill's story:

> Let a wise old man be placed at the door of the monastery, one who knoweth how to take and give an answer, and whose mature age doth not permit him to stray about. The porter should have a cell near the door, that they who come may always find one present from whom they may obtain an answer. (*Holy*)

Father Porter does not quite have the quietude of mind to make him a suitable porter. He is too much connected to the world below, too willing to engage with ideas he should not, given his vows and commitment to the monastery, and yet is transported by the vision, real or not, of the Virgin Mary coming on her "Son's business."

Perhaps, though, that is the point—the miracle in all of these stories lies in the interpretation, not the facts, of the episode. Dana Greene defines this moment in Underhill's fiction as a search for the supernatural: "that which is sought and loved but not known and possessed; that which is beyond but embodied in the ordinary; that which is most accessible in beauty and nature" (Greene 19). Certainly, this story, through the entirely subjective experience of Father Porter, fits Greene's categorization well. Father Porter continues his devotion to the vision at the gate believing for the rest of his days that his encounter was with Mary, mother of Jesus, long after the rest of his colleagues had a good laugh and went back about their business.

THE LADY POVERTY

(*Immanence* 42)

I met her on the Umbrian hills:
    Her hair unbound, her feet unshod.
As one whom secret glory fills
    She walked, alone with God.

I met her in the city street:
    Oh, changed was her aspect then!
With heavy eyes and weary feet
    She walked alone, with men.

* * *

Outro: Heavy Eyes and Weary Feet

The thread that runs through many of Underhill stories and poems of this era may be discerned by her understanding of the word "poverty." Certainly this poem, with its singular main character whom we meet in the wild as well as on a city street, is a bit enigmatic. In modern society, poverty is nobody's friend, yet here she is somehow filled with "secret glory" as she walks the Umbrian hills. Her "heavy eyes and weary feet" are familiar elements to city dwellers, but how can she be such a positive character in a different context? The fourth line of each stanza gives a small clue; Underhill is no doe-eyed Romantic, yet there is a strain in her writing of this era that places the experience of the non-human world, especially the wilderness, as closer to the truth than mere city life:

> It is therefore by the withdrawal of your will from its feverish attachment to things, till "they are under thee and thou not under them," that you will gradually resolve the opposition between the recollective and the active sides of your personality. By diligent self-discipline, that mental attitude which the mystics sometimes call poverty and sometimes perfect freedom—for these are two aspects of one thing—will become possible to you. Ascending the mountain of self-knowledge and throwing aside your superfluous luggage as you go, you shall at last arrive at the point which they call the summit of the spirit; where the various forces of your character—brute energy, keen intellect, desirous heart—long dissipated amongst a thousand little wants and preferences, are gathered into one, and become a strong and disciplined instrument wherewith your true self can force a path deeper and deeper into the heart of Reality. (Underhill *Practical* 70-71)

It is a common theme, expressed elsewhere in "The Ivory Tower" and "A Green Mass," a seeker of knowledge must travel. This poem emphasizes the wisdom and transcendence available to the brave few who are willing to travel "past the towns, very far up the river" for enlightenment.

A GREEN MASS

WHEN THE MESSAGE came to me, I went down to the river, and took a boat that I knew of, and went up the stream towards the hills. I went past the wharves of the ships, and past the water-meadows. A fresh breeze was with me, bringing traders up from the sea, and fishing-boats in from the estuary banks. But I went past all these, and past the towns, very far up the river.

It was after many hours that I came to the place I looked for. At the end of a long reach between moorland banks, where the heather blazed more fiercely because the twilight time was near at hand, I saw two black and rounded headlands that stood out from opposite shores. They nearly met, I thought, in mid-stream. But a narrow water-gate was between them; it went thread-like into the heart of hidden country. With that gate I passed abruptly from the wide and serviceable river into another land.

I was in a valley of the hills, filled to the brim with a very quiet and glassy water that mirrored all day the hills, the woods, the infinite sky. It was a place of entire silence.

Small contorted trees strangely alive, strangely unhappy, stood round the margins of the water. They seemed the powerless victims of some intolerable banishment. Far away at the end, the hills approached one another, as if for another and an inner water-gate.

Through that inner gate also I went, and so to a second hidden valley of water, greater and more silent than the first. I am sure the serenity of that place was very seldom broken, so quiet and stately was the quality of its life. It was plain that the writhing trees which peopled the first valley of approach were of another nation than these keepers of the inner court. It ran before me, a very long and shining lake. Its steep converging banks met at a far away point in the heart of the land. And its margins, too, were hid by the trees; the dark and solemn trees that stood bowed like wise women seeking a lost secret in the glassy waters, and the trees that stood beyond them on the higher ground, close set in tiers and all very attent. Their hooded heads seemed instinct with some antique and sylvan wisdom. I fancied deep eyes bent on me as I passed. I had come a long way from the breezy river and the ships.

Now before me were more trees, and these again different; for the green hooded people went not beyond the precincts, but gave way to a severer majesty. A hill of firs, grey and pinnacled, stood at the end of the valley of water. Their fretted crowns climbed mysteriously into the heavens, tall and dim against the sky: a stronghold of some intangible chivalry. Then I knew that I had come nearly to the end of my journey: that I had gone deep into the immemorial country of the woods.

Now as I came from the second gate down this inner water between the hooded watchers, and to the full sight of the hill of the firs, a great cloud of birds rose out of the shadowy woods that were before me with hoarse cries, and wheeled together in the sky and fell down upon the trees like rain. They rose and wheeled and fell in black streams many times, as if in some elaborate and ritual dance. Their harsh concerted cries drowned all the delicate noises of the woods. It was then that I noticed the strange brilliance of the sky behind them: for it was the hour of that evening radiance which gives to a dim world the illusion of infinite light. I was encompassed, it seemed, by still waters and shining sky; by the intent and waiting woods, the black and vivid shapes of wheeling crying birds.

Suddenly all the birds fell down upon the trees together, and vanished amongst the branches, and it was very quiet. The messenger said in my ear, "It is the hour of the rites." I saw the sky like a live flame behind the trees.

So we came to the foot of that city of firs, and left the boat in the court of silent water, and stood on land. But the hill of trees barred the way like a fort. Then there was shown to me a secret path, known to the hidden people of that place, but to none else. And we went between august and slender trees that bent to watch us, and between others that threw out tendrils trying to stop our way, and others again more subtle that opened to us a wrong road between their trunks. But because of the power of the messenger we won past them all; and away from the entanglements to a sudden bare place where the trees stood back, and one might see the brown earth, starred with scented mint, and with spearwort and sweet madder.

Then I looked up, and saw the trees crowding circlewise about me, one behind the other, dense and massy. I became aware of all the forest pressing steadily and anxiously towards this place. But invisible hands kept them back from the ground that I stood upon, as if that spot were too sacred for actual life. I had come to the Amphitheatre of the Woods. I stood back like the rest; and, with all the forest, waited.

Now it seemed that the blazing sky took on a peculiar glory. Scents rose from the dusky ground as of herbs, more precious than the poor mint that grew there, crushed till their essence was poured out upon the air. And an altar was set in the amphitheatre, and before it the fireless smoke of incense went up; and one, of whom I may not speak, came, and stood by that altar. But no *Confiteor* was audibly spoken, and no *Introit* was sung; for these with whom I worshipped do by their act of living confess Him in beauty every hour of the day, standing always in His presence.

And I turned and saw them all assembled to the sacrifice. Yes! And not the great presences of the forest only; the deep-eyed elementals and the wild and airy fauns who watch us from the thicket; but all the humble furry timid creatures, the smallest and simplest of the children of God; flying and creeping things that live securely hidden in the branches; burrowing things held warm in the bosom of the earth. All the population of the woods had come to do honour to the rite. These were silent; but far away behind the trees, one sang—a wordless *Gloria* full of wild fervours, a passionate invocation of the Light of the Word.

For them what Gradual would avail, what Song of Ascents? I heard then the agony of the natural world as it climbed the steep stairway towards God. The antique wisdom of the forest cried its *Credo*, made itself an oblation to the highest; and when the great ones were silent, the low wail of the wind in the branches took their words, and murmured: *Suscipe, sancte Pater!* ["Accept, O holy Father!"] But he who stood at the altar made no sign.

Only more spices were thrown upon the censer, and

small cleansing flames sprang up within the smoke. It was by fire that the elements were blessed. When they had passed through those flames, something of the earth-sorcery stood purged and white beyond the threshold. It was known then that a certain hope had been administered, a promise of healing given. All about me voices rose up—faint voices of the little things, and the strong and urgent cries of the greater powers; and some, more terrible, out of the darkness of the deeper woods. All the air was full of wings, and of the cry of distant waters. It was thus that the *Sanctus* was sung by the people of the forest:—*Vere dignum et justum est!* ["It is truly meet and just."]

But when they had come to the end of the hymn, as the woods sank again to quietness, there came tearing and rending sounds from the thicket, and one sprang out and stood alone in the green circle. He seemed driven to that place by the pricking of an irresistible desire. I saw the cleft feet, the shagged limbs, and the greatness of his stature; but his face I could not see. He knelt on the ground and kissed the earth. When he spoke, fear fell on all the little waiting creatures.

And he said in a loud voice, *Benedictus qui venit in nomine Domini!* ["Blessed is he who comes in the name of the Lord."] And instantly he who stood by the altar cried *Te igitur, clementissime Pater!* ["To you, therefore, most merciful Father!"] And the rite went on whilst that terrible penitent knelt upon the threshold, and all the people of the forest stood silently in their place.

It was thus that a secret sacrifice was offered, and an incredible oblation made. Not only for the great dwellers in the woodland was the Immortal Victim offered up, but for the small and the helpless also; those little ones slain every hour of the day, the small cry of whose torment ascends incessantly to heaven. The hooded sorceresses drew nearer, and their deep eyes were fixed upon the altar. I heard the branches of the trees sway gently under the movement of the birds. Except for the hushed voice of the Celebrant there was no other sound in the forest. The fire in the sky grew faint; there was dimness in the Amphitheatre of the Woods; the smoke of incense lay across the place in blue folds like a veil.

Strange elements were offered; even those that had passed through the flame and put on a new vesture in the passing. New names were given to them, and very holy powers. I knew of that mystical Passion by which the natural order, no less than the restricted church of man, seeks reconciliation with the Light:—*Unde et memores, Domine, nos serve tui, sed et plebs tua sancta.* ["Wherefore, O Lord, we Thy servants, as also Thy holy people."] An inconceivable presence came to the sanctuary of the woods; an awful substitution was commemorated; a secret consolation drew near. There came a moment when the penitent upon the threshold lay prostrate, and when that messenger who had brought me to this place said:—"Look not, for it is forbidden." But I thought there were sounds of weeping, and presently I knew that a great peace came and brooded over the forest.

And it was known that though Death would continue, and fear also: yet all was well, because Earth had offered the holy atonement with desire and with burning love. So that now every death in the thicket, every agony of the little slain creatures, was a sacrifice willingly made, and endured with good hope; for Earth is saved by pain, and by the torment of her children accomplishes the eternal ritual of sacrifice, ascends into the hill of the holy place. So by the elevation of the Victim was symbolised the raising up of the natural order, and by the drinking of this unnamable Cup, the tasting of that strong potion of eternity which shall be held to the lips of all those who come to the narrow door of the first death.

It was therefore with the great cry of a thankful recognition that the *Agnus* was sung at the consummation of the offering. To these how familiar a rite was the slaying of a humble victim; how divine a hope lay hid in the raising of that diurnal sacrament of nature to the plane of an intercessory gift! I heard the joyful notes of the birds, as they poured out their last oblation. But through these came the strong voice of the penitent; and it was full of the anguish of an unslaked desire, of the cry of the children of the forest as they grope towards the Ineffable Light.

Calicem salutaris accipiam et nomen Domini invocabo! ["I will accept the cup of salvation and will call upon the name of the Lord!"] he cried.

But I saw not that the Cup was indeed vouchsafed to him. Though the sacrifice of the woods be offered for the healing of creation, yet none may come to the communion of that altar save he who intercedes.

So it was that at the ending of the *Agnus* the light was taken from the sanctuary, and from the penitent the immediate hope. All the world of the woods had grown dim. The fire had died from the sky. The altar was cold; it looked white and chill in the darkness. The shadows came round me, and shut me as in a prison of dream; only I apprehended the very gentle steps of the wild creatures who went soft-foot to their homes. The trees drew close, held as I was in the gathering dark; and still I thought that deep eyes gazed from under the green hoods, gazed on the terrible penitent who prayed still for the Cup of Initiation, and on the cold altar whence none replied.

Then the messenger who had summoned me to these rites said in my ear *Ite! Missa est* [Go! The Mass is ended]. And I turned and went back by the secret path and by the quiet water that lies between the watching woods; and by the water-gate to those that stand without, and to the serviceable river. And so back by the breezy reaches to the wharves of the ships, and to the great world.

* * *

Outro: That Daily Crucifixion

In this journey to a strange land so far upstream that even the trees and animals are completely different from those in more familiar places, the main character encounters what Underhill calls "Reality," the truth beyond the veil of the everyday. The main character finds in the rite that takes place among the singing trees and forest denizens access the unprocessed and misinterpreted truths about the nature of reality. The area is populated by creatures from a variety of mythic traditions—"the deep-eyed elementals and the wild and airy fauns"—including a vein of pagan mythology concerning "august and slender trees that bent to watch us." The sentient trees presage Tolkien's ents, who come into being several decades later.

But instead of finding horrors trying to impede the way, the searcher instead finds the Roman Mass played out on this preternatural altar. What might have been a Satanic rite in Dennis Wheatley's *The Devil Rides Out* (1934) or a meeting with the Devil in Nathaniel Hawthorne's "Young Goodman Brown" (1835) turns out to be the Christian rite performed by nature itself. The sacrifice is accompanied by the *Agnus*, the prayer that begins, "Lamb of God, you take away the sins of the world...," signaling the completion of the transformation of the Eucharist, and appropriately connecting the human world to the animal one. The mystical belief is that through this sacrifice, humanity is transported beyond the constructed world it has made to the unseen world that lies beyond. The image also presages C.S. Lewis's depiction of the sacrifice of Aslan in his work of fantasy, *The Lion, the Witch, and the Wardrobe* (1950). In essence, all of the ritual and sacrifice retold by Christianity predates any "civilized" notion of religion.

In her later book, *The Lost Word: A Spiritual Journey* (1907), Underhill recycles "A Green Mass" as the first chapter of the second part of the book entitled "St. Hubert's Way." She recasts the story to be part of a conversation among artists who are rebuilding the edifice of a cathedral. In this chapter, one artist is creating a stained-glass window to depict the story of St. Hubert, while another tells the story in such a beautiful way—using an only slightly edited version of the story that is presented here—that the listeners are transported as if to a higher level of consciousness. St. Hubert is an eighth-century saint who spent his time hunting instead of going to mass, until one day he encounters a stag who has the Crucifix suspended in its antlers. A voice tells him to convert and become a missionary, which he does. It may also be interesting to note that Hubert was her fiancé's name as well.

By having a character narrate the story in the novel, Underhill gives herself room to explain this bizarre plot and its connection to both the Christian rite and to mysticism. Before the story begins, the characters question how deer hunting can lead to a mystical understanding of God. The narrator replies, "There is a secret path there, too, perhaps, which leads to the unnamable rites. There is more than one road, even now; though it needs a fierce desire and an unconquerable will to find it. St. Hubert found it, and it led him to the Everlasting Passion; that daily crucifixion in which the natural world is justified" (152). They compare the story to the quest for the Holy Grail.

This may also be a call back to the "Panic Spirit" that Underhill explored in "The Mountain Image." "Panic" in this case refers not to a heightened emotional state but to the mythical Pan, the god of sensuous delight and chaos. Christopher Armstrong, in his biography of Evelyn Underhill, compares that story to the writings of Arthur Machen. He writes:

> Machen's stories using the notion of panic obsession seem merely "creepy" by comparison, even if one concedes that they are better written. But it is a general rule that where Machen and Evelyn overlap, it is she and not he who gives the impression of deeply exploring the risks and perils of what she somewhere calls "the supersensual life." (Armstrong 50)

While He might have been accusing Underhill of a pantheistic mindset, here she shows how the enduring Christian Mass predates even Christianity and how the civilization that comes with institutional Christianity might be the thing that keeps us from communing with God.

ICHTHUS

(*Immanence* 68–69)

Threatening the sky,
Foreign and wild the sea,
Yet all the fleet of fishers are afloat;
They lie
Sails furled
Each frail and tossing boat,
And cast their little nets into an unknown world.
The countless, darting splendours that they miss,
The rare and vital magic of the main,
The which for all their care
They never shall ensnare—
All this
Perchance in dreams they know;
Yet are content
And count the night well spent
If so
The indrawn net contain
The matter of their daily nourishment.

The unseizable sea,
The circumambient grace of Deity,

Where live and move
Unnumbered presences of power and love,
Slips through our finest net:
We draw it up all wet,
A-shimmer with the dew-drops of that deep.
And yet
For all their toil the fishers may not keep
The instant living freshness of the wave;
Its passing benediction cannot give
The mystic meat they crave
That they may live.

But on some stormy night
We, venturing far from home,
And casting our poor trammel to the tide,
Perhaps shall feel it come
Back to the vessel's side,
So easy and so light
A child might lift,
Yet hiding in its mesh the one desired gift;
That living food
Which man for ever seeks to snatch from out the flood.

* * *

Outro: The Metaphor of the Sea

Fish appear throughout the New Testament and are linked closely with Jesus himself on several occasions. The simple two-arc drawing of a fish was a symbol used by Christians to identify themselves to each other in times of persecution. Even the Greek word for fish, Icthus, itself is an acronym meant to remind Christians of the central tenet of their beliefs, the letters standing for "Jesus Christ, Son of God, Savior," and was a reminder of Jesus's hidden divinity. Underhill's use of this ancient symbol may allude to her participation in a secret society as part of her own burgeoning call to the Christian faith.

In the poem "Clouds," Underhill uses the sea as a metaphor, placing angels above the surface of the water trying to discern human civilization somewhere in the shadowy depths. The roles are reversed. Humans skim along the surface unaware of what occurs below them. We drop our little nets into the sea hoping for sustenance and almost always fail to find it. It is only when we surrender the idea that we are going to ensnare the "mystic meat" that we "crave," only then that we might find what is hidden in our nets is exactly what we've been searching for all along. Even as Jesus recast the metaphor to call his apostles to be "fishers of men" in the Gospel of Mark, Underhill proposes that we could be the fish but we might just as well be the fishers. Our position in the metaphor does not matter as much as our openness to the experience and our willingness to surrender our effort and expectations in a search for meaningfulness.

THE THREEFOLD QUEST

KING MELCHIOR WALKED alone in the hanging gardens that terraced his palace walls. He was very lonely, old, and tired. Desire still lived in him, though its inheritor despair had long been born. He looked out upon the empty desert in which his city was set, and wished for death, for there alone he hoped to find reality. He was King of the Spirit of Man.

He walked the terrace with a certain air of impatience: for midnight was past, and he awaited the rising of the new star which, as he remembered with sardonic pleasure, had upset the calculations of the court astrologer. It shone with a peculiar splendour, and Melchior, who embellished a taste for science with some of the sentiments of an aesthete, felt himself drawn towards it with a rapidly increasing affection. Its light always fell upon a patch of sand, very far away; and it seemed to the king that this spot then became a focus of infinite peace and satisfaction. He had suspected of late that the walls of his comfortable city were barriers, which kept him from this radiant emptiness; where, as he was sure, old age and loneliness would no longer bear the disheartening significance that they had at home, and the profitless wisdom which had made his court a celebrated centre of learning would at last meet the Reality which it sought.

Because he could not bear the long and solitary watch, and the dark, unfriendly sky, he left his terraced garden, and went through sleeping streets to the temple that was in the heart of the town. There an ever-living lamp burned before an empty shrine; for the king had set up many gods only to dethrone them, and the flame and the temple waited a Divine Guest. The place was very dreary, and the dusty symbols which his priests had erected singularly meaningless. It increased his latent longing for great and empty spaces: for the desert, that was less desolate than this admirably appointed sanctuary, and for that object of a limitless adoration which his lonely kingdom could not provide.

He took a censer and lit the coals within it by the flame of the ever-living lamp. The perfume and smoke ascended, wrapped him round, shut him from the world; so that he forgot his kingship and the careful dignities of his little court, and became filled with the ardours of some unknown, incredible quest. He left the temple, and saw the star that he longed for. It had risen over the desert whilst he lingered by the empty shrine. It called to him insistently; and a voice within answered the call. It drew him to a little postern in the walls of his city; and so he left his sleeping kingdom, abruptly almost, and without deliberate intention, and descended by steep paths to the wilderness. As he walked he swung the heavy censer, in long and rhythmic beats. The ascending smoke went before him, a white companionable column full of delicate wreathing shapes. The burning perfume filled the air with strange and elusive desires, dim suggestions of ineffable peace. The hot coals cast a light on his path. He went slowly, for he was very old, and had lost the habit of solitary pilgrimage.

The star stood in mid-heaven. Melchior could no longer see the patch of sand that it lit; but its pale and steady fire drew him, as a lamp set in a window draws the lover across the dark and menacing desert towards some adorable and irresistible event. Because his face was set towards it, and all practical things were left behind, some of the ardours of the lover awoke in him—joy, desire, and unrest. He had forgotten his kingless city on the hill, and the strange folly of this undertaking. He looked with infinite satisfaction on the silent wastes before him, glad to know himself alone.

It was therefore with considerable annoyance that he presently perceived a patch of darkness, which crawled over the face of the desert as clouds crawl over the sky. His solitude was over. There were other wayfarers abroad, fellow-travellers, for the dark patch followed the star; and soon from another quarter came another moving shadow that would join it, and within it the moving lights of many lanterns and the glitter of polished arms. The wilderness, which he had loved for its desolation, teemed with life. King Melchior drew near to the first company, and saw in its midst a great prince surrounded by his escort; tall and dark, the lord of mighty empires. He recognised his neighbour, Balthasar, the King of the Will of Man.

When they were come near enough to hear each other's voice, Balthasar cried, "My cousin, what do you seek?"

Melchior answered, "I seek an escape from life, for it is illusion and weariness. What do you seek, cousin?"

Balthasar replied, "I seek this star, for I am assured that it offers an escape from death, which threatens to destroy me, and with me all my power and joy."

Melchior said, “You believe that you will die? I congratulate you on your good fortune.”

Then he turned, and saw that the third wayfarer had joined them: a pretty youth in fair clothing, who came surrounded by his camels, hounds and horses, his dancing girls and boys. He had great wealth, but little dominion, for he was Caspar, the King of Man’s Body, and Caesar’s feudatory. Melchior said to him with great courtesy, “And what, cousin, do you seek?”

Caspar replied, “Life brings pain, and death takes joy away. I seek in this star the satisfaction of perfect love eternally renewed.”

Then, because their road was the same, though the end of their adventure clearly different, they went on together, and so continued many days; a strange trio, set on a threefold quest. Melchior, the king of one lonely stronghold; Balthasar, who ruled great countries; Caspar, the royal slave. All were stricken with a vague and fevered craving, a dim knowledge of something that they must seek.

And after long while the star led them to the confines of the desert, and they saw a great road which ran away to the horizon, with cornfields and thick woods on either hand. Far off, the black shafts of many mines and factories, the smoke and gloom of human habitations, lay dark in the curve of a hollow valley, and above them very great and awful hills. With the coming of the dawn the star had faded from the sky. There was nothing to guide them in this world.

The King of the Will looked up at the veiled summits of the mountains. “There,” he said, “is the ending of our pilgrimage; for those hidden peaks must dominate the world. There I shall pay my tribute, and be at peace.”

So they went all day upon the road that led to the hills:

past the pleasant woods, and past the fields of hay and green corn. The crested grasses waved in the breeze, offering a scented resting-place. Small enticing paths wandered away to the shaded and flowery forest. Caspar looked at them with regret. The mountains were austere and terrible; as day fell, they took on a peculiar majesty. He feared them; but Balthasar marched with eagerness and determination, as if to the conquest of a desirable kingdom. Melchior went alone, swinging the smoking censer which gave to his journey the air of some secret and mystical rite. The Kings of the Will and the Body smiled at his curious fervour. They perceived him to be an eccentric and possibly senile person, who would have fared ill without their protection on the road.

But when night was come, and they were at the foot of the hills, Balthasar saw with disappointment that the star had turned aside. It shone over the smoky town in the curve of the valley, and was reflected in a thousand twinkling lights.

Caspar said, "It is well! Warmth, joy, and the fulfilment of desire are in the lowlands. There I shall break my jars of myrrh and precious ointment, for the honouring of perfect beauty and the adornment of undying love."

So they followed the star; and it brought them, whilst the night was still dark, to the city, where furnace fires blazed, and hammers rang incessantly upon anvils, and a pall of smoke shut out the sky. The aspect of the place was not encouraging. But they went on, for though its precincts were unlit, the burning coals in Melchior's censer cast a light on the muddy pathway; and presently they were caught in a network of mean streets and dingy tenements, ill-suited to the tastes of royal travellers. Caspar and Balthasar turned this way and that, to find some decent road by which their camels and men-at-arms could pass. Thus, becoming entangled in the narrow courts and alleys, they soon lost one another; and when dawn came, each, looking for his companions, found himself alone amongst an inquisitive and ill-mannered population, which gave more ridicule than reverence to this pilgrimage of strange kings who had come down many worlds and countless centuries on a vague and unpractical quest.

Now, about mid-day the King of the Spirit, having wandered for many hours through the dreary by-ways of a prosperous manufacturing town, came out with a great sense of thankfulness on to the waste ground on the far side of the city. There he found by the roadside the King of the Will, who sat alone under the shadow of a great block of dwellings which was the last outpost of the poorer quarters. There were draggled women and screaming children all about him. He seemed very tired: his torn robes were soiled by the refuse of the streets. He looked at King Melchior, and perceiving that he no longer carried his censer said, "What has happened to you, my cousin, and why did you forsake the quest? I have looked for you all day."

Melchior answered, "I followed the star."

Balthasar said, "That cannot be, for I went with it all night in solitude: and it brought me very early in the morning to the greatest king in all the world, even he who rules over this town."

Melchior replied, "Yet all night I saw it go before me, shining very faintly through the smoke; and it brought me at last to the Ineffable Mystery, which is without doubt the true end of this quest. For after many weary hours, it stayed before a house in a wide street, where there was great business of buying and selling, and a concourse of people going to and fro with must jostling and noise. I knocked, and a man came to the door and took me in; and I saw a table set out with white and shining Bread, and a Cup that was filled with wine like fire. And many poor folk stood round the table, that they might be nourished; and the man of the house gave freely to all. And each, as he ate that Bread and drank of the Cup, left all his pain and unrest, which are but illusion, and opened his eyes on reality and peace. Then I knew that my quest was accomplished, and I knelt, and adored, and received: and so I stayed till the fire in my censer was spent. And after that I came out of the house, the star moved from the door and went before me; and it brought me to this place, whence no doubt I shall return to my kingdom in due time."

Balthasar laughed, and said, "You were deceived, cousin. I too followed the star, and some of my men rode with me. It brought us by sorry places, and past the tavern that you speak of; a foul place it seemed. The man that dwells there came out, and bade us enter. He is a charitable fellow, who nourishes poor travellers with broken victuals. He would have given us a meal of his rye-bread and sour wine; but my men mocked at such entertainment, for we had better things in our saddle-bags. So I rode on, and the star went before me, and when day broke it brought me to an open place in the midst of the city. There I saw a strange sight indeed, and glorious; even a King, who ruled from a Tree. He was poor and mean of aspect, without royal robes or any sign of sovereignty. His limbs were cruelly maimed. Yet he was set high above the earth, that all might do him homage, and none disputed his dignity. When I came near, I saw that he was dead; but none the less he continued his reign. Then I said, 'This is the King of kings whom I seek, for his rule has triumphed over the grave.' And I left my tribute of gold at the foot of the Tree. And when I had so done, the star went on, and brought me out of the town."

Whilst they spoke together, they saw with great surprise the King of the Body, who came out of the many-storied tenement near which they sat. He was alone and empty-handed. He wept as he walked.

The King of the Will said to him with great kindness, "Alas! my poor cousin, you had better have followed the star: for now I perceive that you have lost all and found nought."

Caspar replied, "Not so. The star has been with me, even to this moment; and it has shown me perfect beauty and eternal love, which is the most piteous sight in all the world."

Balthasar said, "What! Beauty in this foul dwelling?"

Caspar answered, "The casket matters little, when one has seen the jewel that it holds."

Melchior said, "By what road did you come?"

Caspar replied, "By many busy streets and by a poor house of refreshment, where the host offered me coarse food, and by the market-place, where a felon hung stark upon the gallows. And my pages and dancing girls were weary and frightened, and lagged behind, so that at last I lost them all in the tangle of the streets, and found myself alone. And a little after dawn, when the star was very faint and hard to see, it brought me to the door of this tenement. I went in, and climbed many stairs. I heard a sound of bitter weeping, that grew louder as I climbed; till I came at last to a little attic, and there I saw a marvellous Child, which lay dead on its mother's knee. She wept, and her tears fell down on its white body like diamonds upon snow. I said to her, 'Who is this child, and why is he so beautiful? For he is formed like a king's son.' She answered, 'He is the fruit of perfect love. With pain he was born, and with pain he was taken away.' Then I knew I had found that which I sought, the beauty which is eternally renewed: and I broke my jar of myrrh and anointed that perfect little body for its burial, weeping because I had seen the fulfilment of desire, which is the child of love and pain. And when I had so done, the star moved from that place and brought me here."

King Melchior smiled, and said, "You have behaved with much condescension. As for me, I dislike the children of the poor. They disturb my meditations."

Balthasar retorted, "Yet you found the food of poverty strangely sweet."

Melchior answered, "At least I did not mistake a felon for my king, nor a pauper woman's grief for perfect love."

Thus they sat and disputed, and cloaked their very natural anxiety with recriminations: for their servants were lost, and their beasts, and all provision for the homeward journey, and they found themselves reduced to the condition of any poor pilgrims on the road. Each believed in his heart that he had achieved the quest, and was eager to return to his kingdom; but without the guidance of the star they could not find the way. Each was very sorry for his companions, knowing that they had mistaken the sign and been duped by vulgar deceits.

But the star did not move. It stood with singular obstinacy above the thatch of a miserable outhouse that was by the wayside, and shone with ever-increasing splendour on the briars and brambles which grew over its door. And whilst they waited, very hungry and disconsolate, a messenger came and stood before them, and said, "Will you not come in?"

They said, "Where would you take us?"

He answered, "To that which you seek."

Each replied quickly, "But I have found!"

The messenger said, "No! for that which you found was Three, but the consummation of the quest is One."

Then the three kings were full of distress, saying, "Alas! it is too late, for we came on this adventure bearing rich gifts to him whom we sought, but now all that we have is spent, and we are empty-handed as the poor. It is not fitting that we should come in."

The messenger answered, "What gifts did you bring?"

Melchior said, "I bore incense to the God."

The messenger replied, "Its perfume is yet about His feet."

Balthasar said, "I brought tribute to the King."

The messenger replied, "At daybreak it was laid before His throne."

Caspar said, "I brought myrrh to the Man."

The messenger replied, "Even now it was poured out upon His limbs."

And he went before them to the little outhouse on which the star still cast its light. And they were greatly displeased at it, for they were heartily tired of the sight of squalid dwellings, and this was a shelter ill-suited indeed to mighty kings. Nevertheless for very weariness they followed him: and seeing it now to be all grown about with fragrant roses, that shone like living flames by the light of the star, each said in his heart, "Without doubt this is an hallucination produced by excessive fatigue; for we are yet upon the edge of the city, and this place is but an outhouse where drovers coming to market herd their beasts." The King of the Spirit was forced to stoop low that he might pass under its lintel; so low, that the briars which grew across it did not touch him at all, only a rose brushed his forehead very softly as he passed. The King of the Will and the King of the Body came after; but because Balthasar stood very tall and stooped not, he was compelled to remove his crown before he could go in, and the briars that hung below the lintel checked Caspar's hasty entrance, and tore his brow.

But when they were come in, they forgot straightway all their weariness and the miseries and illusions of the way; being seized by the passions of adoration and service and love. For the beams of the star lit the place with a light that was exceeding sweet and glorious. And there they found Mary, and Joseph, and the Babe.

* * *

Outro: The Passions of Adoration and Service and Love

On one hand, this short story has all the trappings of a fairly conventional story about the visit of the three wise men to the site of the birth of Jesus, the story that first appeared in the Gospel of Matthew. Longstanding Christian tradition has three wise men who follow the light of a star across the desert to Bethlehem where they bestow their curious gifts and alert King Herod about a new threat to his throne. The names of the three Magi also derive from longstanding tradition. Although they are not named in Matthew's account, by the eighth century they had acquired the names that Underhill uses possibly from a lost sixth-century Greek source. The three wise men are motivated by different reasons, and yet they travel together and arrive simultaneously to the humble location where Mary and Joseph have become parents.

A deeper reading, however, reveals the strangeness at the center of this story. In previous stories, we've seen

Underhill's inclination to make available the experience of the mystical and strange to anyone whose heart is open to it. She is getting closer and closer to 1911 when *Mysticism* will be published, and so the emphasis in her fiction on the lone mystic raving on the outskirts of society has waned. In "Mountain Image," Underhill shows us a character who has seen beyond the veil, but cannot alter his childhood vision of the world beyond and so is destroyed. The experience is overwhelming, and the human consciousness is ill-equipped to witness the reality of the universe. In "The Threefold Quest," each king sees reality from his own subjective perspective, and when they compare their experiences, they do not match up, causing each to be dissatisfied.

Reality has been trisected as the story opens, with the Wise Men from the Gospel of Matthew each stirring themselves in response to the appearance of the strange star. These three kings represent the three aspects of fallen humanity. Melchior is "King of the Spirit of Man" and searches for a way to defeat death. Balthasar is "King of the Will of Man," and his quest is an escape from the illusion and weariness of life. Caspar is "King of Man's Body," and he searches for "perfect love eternally renewed." In splitting human existence into three pieces—mind, body, and spirit—Underhill participates in the Neoplatonic tradition that explored ideas about dualism in describing human existence. She also evokes the Christian doctrine of the Trinity: the threefold nature of the one God as incarnate in the Father, Son, and Holy Spirit. For St. Augustine, this idea of trinity manifested itself in the memory, intelligence, and will of humans, a parallel to what Underhill seems to be working with in creating her three Magi. The tripling continues right up to the end of the story, where the three travelers "forgot straightway all their weariness and the miseries and illusions" and were taken by "the passions of adoration and service and love" just before they "found Mary, and Joseph, and the Babe."

A DEFENCE OF MAGIC

I.

THE GRADUAL DEBASEMENT of the verbal currency results in many regrettable misconceptions. Of these, perhaps none provides so constant an irritant for the student of mysticism as the loss of the true meaning of the word Magic. Magic, in the vulgar tongue, means the art practised by Mr. Maskelyne. The shelf which is devoted to its literature in the London Library contains many useful works on sleight-of-hand and parlour tricks. It has dragged with it in its fall the terrific verb, "to conjure," which, forgetting that it once compelled the spirits of men and angels, is now content to produce rabbits from top-hats.

Yet the real significance of these words should hardly be lost in a Christian country; for Magic is the science of those Magi whose quest of the symbolic Blazing Star brought them to the cradle of the Incarnate God. This science does not consist in the production of marvels. Its true adepts have always condemned necromancy, fortune-telling, and other devices for the astonishment of the crowd. It is a living and serious philosophy, descended from immemorial antiquity, and never failing of initiates, who have handed down to the present day its secret wisdom, symbols and speculations.

There was a schoolmaster who said to his construing class, "Remember that the Latin poets did not invariably write nonsense." So, it seems necessary to remind the present generation, weighed down as we are by a sense of our own perspicacity, that the occult philosophers, from Empedocles to Paracelsus, were great personalities, who exercised a commanding influence over the minds with which they came in contact. Throughout the long and tangled history of "the science of the charlatan" discerning students may perceive a thread of gold, never lost though often concealed, which links the hidden wisdom of the ancient with the profoundest speculations of the modern schools. This thread is the true "tradition of magic"; originating in the East, formulated and preserved in the religion of Egypt. In Gnosticism, in the Hebrew Kabala, in much of the ceremonial of the Christian religion, and finally in secret associations which still exist in most European countries, the "thread of gold" has wandered down the centuries. These things have kept alive, if not intact, a philosophy which, like religion, has been always misunderstood by the unworthy majority, but remains a source of illumination to the few. It is this philosophy which I propose to defend; and because the quaint fine trappings of "far-off forgotten things" are apt to offer careless readers the picturesqueness of cloak and feathers instead of the living organism which these things clothe, I will examine it first as exhibited in the writings and in the experience of an eminently sane French philosopher of the nineteenth century. This writer found in the magical tradition, rehandled in the terms of modern thought, an adequate theory of the universe and rule of practical life. He thus forms a link between our time and that of his teachers, the Kabalists and Hermetic philosophers of the Middle Ages.

Alphonse Louis Constant, well known under his fantastic pseudonym of Eliphas Lévi, was born in France about the year 1810. He was a shoemaker's son; but his unusual intelligence obtained for him an education at the seminary of St. Sulpice, where he received minor orders. Constant's eager mind, at once critical and visionary, could not rest in the arid formularism of the French Catholic theology of his day. He made the inevitable pilgrimage of the youthful individualist from orthodoxy to Voltarian agnosticism, was expelled from St. Sulpice, and passed under the influence of a political illuminist name Esquiros, who announced himself as an initiate of occult science. Possibly Constant obtained from Esquiros his first introduction to magic: if this be so, the pupil soon excelled his master. During these *Wanderjahre* he made a romantic but unhappy marriage, his wife finally deserting him, to his great grief. It is perhaps not unreasonable to trace a connection between these events and the turning of Eliphas Lévi's mind towards those speculations which afterwards dominated his life.

The date at which he embraced Hermetic philosophy is obscure; but in 1853 he was already skilled in magic, and well known to its serious students. In this year he came to England, and there performed the amazing ceremonial evocation of Apollonius of Tyana which he describes in his most celebrated work, the *Dogme de la Haute Magie.* This extraordinary narrative is like a wizard's tale of the Middle Ages reported by the Society for Psychical Research. Nothing can be more curious than its blend of the mystical, scientific, and bizarre. The assignation with an unknown old lady outside Westminster Abbey; the "completely equipped magician's cabinet," which she promptly places at Constant's disposal, with its altars, mirrors, perfumes, and pentagrams; the twenty-one days of preparation for the rite. Then the evocation: Constant crowned with vervain leaves and clothed in a white magician's robe, reciting antique ritual, and, in a true scientific spirit, checking his own sensations at each point in the ceremony. His attitude at the beginning of the adventure is not that of a mystic seeking transcendental truth; it is that of a victim of intense intellectual curiosity. Nevertheless, the ceremony produced its traditional effect. A phantom appeared; vague at first, but afterwards distinct. Many ordinary spiritualistic phenomena accompanied the evocation: the sense of fear, of intense cold. The hand by which Constant held the magic sword was touched and benumbed from the shoulder, and so remained for many days. At the third evocation he became exhausted, and sank into a condition of coma; but on his awakening, he found that the questions he had desired to ask the phantom had answered themselves "within his own mind" during the period of unconsciousness.

Though he refused to acknowledge it probable, or even possible, that he had really evoked and seen the spirit of Apollonius of Tyana, this vision was for Constant a crucial experience, and left behind it marked physical and mental effects. "*Je n'explique pas*," he says, "*par quelles lois physiologiques j'ai vu et touché; j'affirme seulement que j'ai vu et que j'ai touché, que j'ai vu clairement et distinctement, sans rêves, et cela suffit pour croire à l'efficacité réelle des cérémonies magiques.*"[1] Again, "*L'effet de cette expérience sur moi fut quelque chose d'inexplicable. Je n'étais plus le même homme, quelque chose*

[1] "I do not explain the physical laws by which I saw and touched; I affirm solely that I did see and that I did touch, that I saw clearly

d'un autre monde avait passé en moi; je n'étais plus ni gai, ni triste, mais j'éprouvais un singulier attrait pour la mort, sans être, cependant, aucunement tenté de recourir au suicide"[2] (*Dogme de la Haute Magie*, pp. 270-271).

Reading this passage, it is difficult to avoid the conclusion that, owing perhaps to the ecstasy produced by the perfumes, the ritual, the solitude, acting on an eager imagination, there happened to Constant in the course of this experience one of those sudden uprushes from the subliminal consciousness which underlie the phenomena of conversion. It marks, in all probability, its writer's real, as apart from his merely intellectual, initiation into the spirit of occult philosophy.

It is during the decade 1855-1865, corresponding roughly with the period of Eliphas Lévi's literary activity, that we can best observe that mental evolution which is so candidly reflected in his writings. The first part of his great work upon Hermetic science, the *Dogme de la Haute Magie*, was issued in 1854, and its sequel, the *Rituel*, in 1856. In 1860 appeared the *Histoire de la Magie: La Clef des Grands Mystères*, which completes the trilogy, following in 1861, and *La Science des Esprits*—a violent condemnation of popular spiritualism—in 1865. During the remainder of his life, Constant wrote much, but published nothing. His pupils have, however, issued many of his MSS. and letters since his death in 1875. Hence there is considerable material available

---

and distinctly, apart from dreaming, and this is sufficient to establish the real efficacy of magical ceremonies." (Lévi *Transcendental* 125)

[2] "The consequence of this experience on myself must be called inexplicable. I was no longer the same man; something of another world had passed into me; I was no longer either sad or cheerful, but I felt a singular attraction towards death, unaccompanied, however, by any suicidal tendency." (Lévi *Transcendental* 125)

for the student who desires to investigate. Eliphas Lévi's spiritual pilgrimages.

He died in complete communion with that Catholic Church from which he had set out in his youth: to which his subsequent adventures, rightly understood, constituted a gradual and consistent return. He has some claim to be included in the ranks of her great apologists; for his works demonstrate, with uncompromising clearness, the fundamental identity of all religious and philosophic truth with that esoteric mystery which dogmatic Catholicism at once veils and reveals. "*Les cultes changent, et la religion est toujours la même*," he says in his posthumous *Livre des Splendeurs*.

This sameness, this One, he at last attained; only to be taunted, by those still entangled amongst the Many, with the obvious insincerity of such a reconciliation with the Church. But to the unprejudiced mind, this reconciliation appears as the inevitable end, for him, of the journey on which he set out. The spectacle presented to us is that of a man of eager desires and natural intuitions pursuing the one eternal quest by strange paths, but with a passionate sincerity. It matters little what road such adventurers choose; whether they seek the symbolic perfection of the Magnum Opus or the Grand Arcanum of the Cross. The end which these things veil is always one. This truth Constant apprehended. It forms the justification of his philosophy and the coping-stone of his work: a work full of fantasy and not guiltless of perversity, yet, as he proudly proclaims on the title-page of the *Histoire de la Magie, Opus hierarchicum et Catholicum*.

II.

Let us now consider the principles of High Magic, as we find them formulated in Eliphas Lévi's works.

Like the world which it professes to interpret, Magic has a body and a soul; an external system of words and ceremonies, and an inner doctrine. The external system—which is all that the word Magic connotes for the average man—is hardly attractive to educated minds. It consists of a series of confusing and ridiculous veils: pretended miracles, absurd if literally understood, strange words and numbers, personifications and mystifications, clearly designed for the bewilderment of impatient investigators. Stripped of these archaic mystery-mongerings, delightful to the aesthetic sense of the adept but exasperating to the ignorant inquirer, true Magic rests on two dogmas, neither of which can be dismissed as absurd by respectful admirers of the amazing hypotheses of fashionable psychology and physics. The first dogma affirms the existence of an imponderable medium or "universal agent," beyond the plane of our normal sensual perceptions, which interpenetrates and binds up the material world. For this medium Lévi borrowed from the Martinists the rather unfortunate name of Astral Light: a term to which the religious rummage-sales of current Theosophy have given a familiarity which treads upon the margin of contempt.

The Astral Light possesses, nevertheless, a respectable ancestry. It is identical with the "ground of the soul" of religious mysticism, with the Azoth which the Spiritual Alchemists call "the First Matter of the Great Work," and with the "Burning Body of the Holy Ghost" of Christian Gnosticism. From it came the Odic Force of old-fashioned spiritualists, and the Vril of Lord Lytton's "Coming Race." According to the doctrine of Magic, the Astral Light is a storehouse of forces more powerful than those which we know upon the physical plane. Intensely receptive, it provides that moral and intellectual "atmosphere" of which many are conscious, and also constitutes the "cosmic memory" in which the images of all beings and events are preserved, as they are preserved in the memory of man. On this theory, spiritualists, evoking the phantoms of the dead, merely call them up from the recesses of universal instead of individual remembrance. Further, the Astral Light is first cousin to the ether of Sir Oliver Lodge, and is the vehicle of telepathy, clairvoyance, and all those supra-normal phenomena which science has taken out of the hands of the occultists and re-named "meta-psychic." Modern psychology, it is plain, can ill afford to sneer at the first principle of Magic.

Occult philosophy has always proclaimed its knowledge of this medium: postulating it as a scientific fact susceptible of verification by the trained powers of the initiate. The possessor of such powers, not the wizard or fortune-teller, is the true magician; and it is the first object of occult education, or "initiation," to establish a conscious communion with this supersensual plane of experience, imposing upon its forces the directive force of the will, as easily as we impose that will upon the "material" things of sense.

Hence the second axiom of Magic, which has also a curiously modern air; for it postulates simply the limitless power of such a disciplined will. This dogma has lately been "taken over" without acknowledgment from occult philosophy, to become the trump card of Christian Science and "New Thought." The ingenious authors of *Volo, The Will to be Well*, and *Just How to Wake the Solar Plexus*, have some of the pure gold of the Magi concealed amongst the strange trappings of their faiths.

The first lesson of the would-be Magus is self-mastery. "*Au moyen d'une gymnastique persévérante et graduée*," says Lévi, "*les forces et l'agilité du corps se développent ou se créent dans une proportion qui étonne. Il en est de même des puissances de l'âme. Voulez-vous régner sur vous-mémes et sur les autres? Apprenez à vouloir. Comment peut-on apprendre à vouloir? Ici est le premier arcane de l'initiation magique*"[3] (*Rituel*, p. 35).

In essence, then, magical initiation is a traditional form of mental discipline, strengthening and focussing the will, by which those powers which lie below the threshold of ordinary consciousness are liberated, and enabled to report their discoveries to the active and sentient mind. This discipline, like that of the religious life, consists partly in physical austerities and in a deliberate divorce from the world, partly in the cultivation of will-power, but largely in a yielding of the mind to the influence of suggestions which have been selected and accumulated in the course of ages because of their power over that imagination which Eliphas Lévi calls "The eye of the soul." There is nothing supernatural about it. It is character-building with an object, conducted upon a heroic scale. In Magic, the uprushes of thought, the abrupt intuitions, which reach us from the subliminal region, are developed and controlled by rhythms and symbols which have become traditional because the experience of centuries has proved their efficacy.

This is the truth hidden beneath the apparently absurd rituals of preparation, the doctrines of signs and numbers, pentacles, charms, and the rest. It is known amongst the

[3] "By means of persevering and graduated athletics, the powers and activities of the body can be developed to an astonishing extent. It is the same with the powers of the soul. Would you reign over yourselves and others? Learn how to will. How can one learn to will? This is the first arcanum of magical initiation [...]" (Lévi *Transcendental* 205)

Indian mystics, who recognise in the *Mantra*, or occult and rhythmic formula, an invaluable help to the attainment of ecstatic states. It again appears in the new American "mysticism," as the necessary starting point of efficacious meditation. It is the practical reason of that need of a formal liturgy which is felt by nearly every organic religion. The true "magic word," or spell, is untranslatable, because its power resides only partially in that outward sense which is apprehended by the intellect, but chiefly in the *rhythm*, which is addressed to the subliminal mind. Did the Catholic Church choose to acknowledge a law long known to the Magicians, she has here an explanation of that instinct which has caused her to cling so strenuously to a Latin liturgy, much of whose amazing—and truly magic—power would evaporate were it translated into the vulgar tongue. Symbols, religious and other, and the many symbolic acts which appear meaningless when judged by the reason alone, perform a similar office.

"*Toutes ces dispositions de nombres et de caractères,*" says Lévi [i.e., sacred words, pentacles, ceremonial gestures], "*ne sont, comme nous l'avons déjà dit, que des instruments d'éducation pour la volonté, dont ils fixent et déterminent les habitudes. Ils servent en outre à rattacher ensemble, dans l'action, toutes les puissances de l'âme humaine, et à augmenter la force créatrice de l'imagination*"[4] (*Rituel*, p. 71).

Magic symbols, therefore, from votive candles to Solomon's Seal, fall, in modern technical language, into two classes. The first class contains instruments of self-suggestion

[4] "All these figures, with the acts analogous thereto, all these dispositions of numbers and of characters, are, as we have said, so many instruments for the education of the will, by fixing and determining its habits. They serve, furthermore, to combine all powers of the human soul in action and to increase the creative force of imagination." (Lévi *Transcendental* 226).

and will direction. To this belong spells, charms, rituals, perfumes, the magician's vervain wreath and burning ambergris, and the "Youth! Health! Strength!" which the student of New Thought repeats when she is brushing her hair in the morning. The second class contains *autoscopes*: *i.e.*, material objects which focus and express the subconscious perceptions of the operator. The dowser's divining rod, fortune-teller's cards, and crystal gazer's ball are characteristic examples. Both kinds are rendered necessary rather by the disabilities of the human, than by the peculiarities of the superhuman plane; and the great adept, like the great saint, may attain heights at which he can entirely dispense with these "outward and visible signs."

These things, now commonplaces of psychology, have been known to students of Magic for countless generations. Those who decry the philosophy because of the absurdity of the symbols should remember that the embraces, gestures, grimaces, and other "ritual acts" by which we all concentrate, liberate, and express love, wrath, and enthusiasm will—when divorced from their inspiring emotions—ill endure a strictly rational examination.

To the two dogmas of the Universal Agent and the power of the will there is to be added a third, that of Analogy, or of implicit correspondence between the seen and unseen worlds. In this, occultism finds the basis of its transcendental speculations. *Quod superius sicut quod inferius*—the first words of that Table of Emerald, which ranks as the magician's Table of Stone —is an axiom which must be agreeable to all Platonists. Truly catholic in the breadth of its application, it embraces alike the visible world, which thus becomes the mirror of the invisible; the parables and symbols of religion; and the creations of musicians, painters, poets.

"*L'analogie*," says Lévi, "*est le dernier mot de la science et le premier mot de la foi ... le seul médiateur possible entre le visible et l'invisible, entre le fini et l'infini*"[5] (*Dogme*, p. 361).

This vital quality and illuminating power of analogy crops up in many unexpected places. It is present of necessity in every perfect work of art. It permeates all the great periods of English literature. Sir Thomas Browne spoke for more than himself when he said, in a well-known passage of the *Religio Medici*: "The severe schools shall never laugh me out of the philosophy of Hermes, that this visible world is but a picture of the invisible, wherein, as in a portrait, things are not truly, but in equivocal shapes, and as they counterfeit some real substance in that invisible fabric."

Our best critics are at one with the magicians in proclaiming its importance. "Intuitive perception of the hidden analogies of things," says Hazlitt, in *English Novelists*, "or, as it may be called, his *instinct of the imagination*, is perhaps what stamps the character of genius on the productions of art more than any other circumstance."

Comparing these passages with Lévi's already quoted dicta, we perceive that there are several senses in which it may be said that the keys of Magic open doors from the Many to the One.

The central doctrine of Magic may therefore be summed up thus:—

(a) That an intangible and real Cosmic medium exists, which interpenetrates, influences, and supports the tangible and apparent world.

(b) That there is an established analogy and equilibrium

[5] "Analogy is the final word of science and the first word of faith... the sole possible mediator between the finite and the infinite." (Lévi *Transcendental* 179)

between this unseen world and the illusory manifestations which we call the world of sense.

(c) That this analogy may be discerned and this equilibrium controlled, by the disciplined will of man, which thus becomes master of itself, and to a certain degree director of its fate.

I submit that these conclusions cannot be dismissed by any student of idealism as vain and foolish inventions.

The third dogma of Magic, torn from its frame, is now recognised as a factor in religion and in therapeutics: our newest theories on these subjects being merely the old Hermetic wine in new bottles. The methods of the magical physician differ in nothing but splendour of ceremonial from those of the modern mental healer.

"*Toute la puissance du médecin occulte,*" says Lévi, "*est dans la conscience de sa volonté, et tout son art consiste à produire la foi dans son malade*"[6] (*Rituel*, p. 312).

This simple truth was in the possession of the magi at a time when Church and State saw no alternative but the burning or beatification of its practitioners. Now, under the polite names of mental hygiene, suggestion, and psycho-therapeutics, it is steadily advancing to the front rank of medical shibboleths. Yet it is still the same "Magic art" which has been employed for centuries by the adepts of Hermetic science.

Again, the accredited psychological theory of religious "experience" rests upon the assumption that by self-suggestion, by the will-to-believe, by "recollection," and other means, it is possible to shift the threshold of consciousness, and to exhibit supranormal powers and perceptions which

[6] "The whole power of the occult physician is in the consciousness of his will, while the whole art consists in exciting the faith of his patient." (Lévi *Transcendental* 365)

are variously attributed to inspiration and to disease. This is exactly what ceremonial magic professes, in milder and more picturesque language, to do for her initiates:—

"*Les opérations magiques ... sont le résultat d'une science et d'une habitude qui exaltent la volonté humaine au-dessus de ses limites habituelles*"[7] (*Rituel*, p. 32).

Recipes for this exaltation of personality and for that opening up of the subliminal field which accompanies it—concealed from the profane by a mass of confusing allegories and verbiage—form the back-bone of all grimoires and occult rituals. The Magi, psychologists before their time, were perfectly aware that ceremony has no objective importance except in its effect upon the operator's mind. In order that this effect may be enhanced, it is given an atmosphere of intensest mystery and sacredness, its rules are strict, its higher arcana difficult of attainment. The arduous preparations and strange rites of an evocation have power, not over the spirits of the dead, but over the consciousness of the living, who is thus caught up from the world of sense to a new plane of perception. For him, not for unknown Presences, are these splendours and arts displayed. No philosophy ever said more plainly to its initiates "The Spirit of God is within you." Thus the whole education of the genuine occult student tends to awake in him a new vision and a new attitude; altering the constituents of that apperceiving mass by which ordinary men are content to know and judge the—or rather *their*—universe.

Finally—in spite of the consistent employment by all great adepts of their "occult power" in the healing of disease—Magic, like Christianity, combines a practical policy

[7] "Magical operations are...the result of a science and a practice which exalt human will beyond its normal limits." (Lévi *Transcendental* 203-204)

of pity for the sick with a creed of suffering and renunciation. Eliphas Lévi, whilst advising the initiate whose conscious will has reached its full strength to employ his powers in the alleviation of pain and prolongation of life, laughs at the student who seeks in Magic a method of escaping suffering or of satisfying his own desires. None, he says, know better than the true magician that suffering is of the essence of the world-plan.

"*Malheur à l'homme qui ne sait pas et qui ne veut pas souffrir, car il sera écrasé de douleurs*"[8] (*Histoire*, p. 36). And again, perhaps his finest single utterance, "*Apprendre à souffrir, apprendre à mourir, c'est la gymnastique de l'Eternité, c'est le noviciat immortel*"[9] (*Ibid.*, p. 147).

So much for that pure Theory of Magic of which Eliphas Lévi is the greatest modern exponent. In his works, its doctrines are seen "through a temperament," and transfigured, perhaps even distorted, in the process. But this is true of every philosophy and religion which man undertakes to interpret to man. It is impossible to deal here with the criticism to which he has been subjected by students of his system, of whom the eminent occultist, Mr. A. E. Waite, must be reckoned as chief. These criticisms, in so far as they are destructive, would appear generally to arise: first, from the natural annoyance which is aroused in any school by the proceedings of a born "free lance"; next from an angry inability to comprehend Lévi's return to the Church of Rome; finally, from a misunderstanding of the degree of reality which he attributed to the symbolic framework on

[8] "Woe to him who cannot and will not suffer; he shall be overwhelmed by pain." (Lévi *History* 32)

[9] "Learn how to suffer and learn also to die—such are the gymnastics of eternity and such is the immortal novitiate." (Lévi *History* 142)

which he wove his deep speculations upon God and the soul. These symbols—drawn chiefly from the Kabala, the Tarot, and mediaeval Alchemy—had, as he progressed, less and less objective importance for him. They were his "ladder to the stars." He was born upon the earth, crying, like the figures in Blake's design, "I want! I want!" By this ladder he, like many other adepts before him, attained something of that which he desired.

He found in the exalted imagery of the Hebrew Kabala the best symbolic expression of Magical philosophy: but he found the final satisfaction of that thirst which Magic had awakened in the mysteries of the Catholic religion. This, it would seem, was the logical result of his progress from a merely intellectual and agnostic to an implicit and spiritual understanding of Hermetic science. It is the defect of all modern occultism that it is tainted by a certain intellectual arrogance. A divorce has been effected between knowledge and love, between the religion and the science of the Magi; and, in the language of mysticism, till these be reunited the Divine Word cannot be born. Eliphas Lévi came to a point at which this was brought home to him; when he saw that "*L'étude approfondie des mystères de la nature peut éloigner de Dieu l'observateur inattentif, chez qui la fatigue de l'esprit paralyse les élans du coeur*"[10] (*Histoire*, p. 541). He perceived that Catholic symbolism, though he believed it to be misunderstood by its official keepers (and "*l'intelligence des symboles est toujours calomniatrice*") might well be the revealing medium of those eternal truths which transcendental magic had always possessed but was no longer able to convey. There, at any rate, place was provided for the "élans du coeur," in

10 "The profound study of natural mysteries may alienate the casual observer from God because mental fatigue paralyses the aspirations of the heart." (Lévi *History* 512)

which the spirit of man pierces furthest into the unknown. In Catholicism he found, as in Magic, the same qualities of purity and detachment, faith, steadfastness, and self-control, accomplishing the same task: that, namely, of opening the eyes of the soul and passing "beyond the flaming rampart of the world." In Magic he found an explanation of those age-old mysteries which are concealed beneath the dogmas of the Church; a reasonable theory of her sacraments and ceremonies: a reconciling medium between philosophy and orthodox faith.

That Christianity, heir of all wisdom and truth, is also the heir of the Magi; that current theology veils, as popular Magic veils, the same ineffable truths, is Lévi's final position. It is a position which is not without justification. All rituals and ceremonies, whatever explanations of their efficacy may be offered by their official apologists, have, and must have, as the *rationale* of their existence, a magical—*i.e.*, a hypnotic—character; and all persons who are naturally drawn towards ceremonial religion are in this respect really devotees of Magic. Sacraments, however simple their beginnings, tend, as they evolve, to assume a magical aspect. Those who observe with understanding, for instance, the Roman rite of baptism, with its spells and exorcisms, its truly hermetic employment of salt, anointing chrism, and ceremonial lights, must see in it a ceremony nearer to the beneficent operations of white magic, than to the simple lustrations practised by Saint John the Baptist.

In the liturgies of the great Eastern and Western churches the occult elements—however we may choose to account for their presence—are peculiarly well marked. Here are sacred numbers, perfumes, invocations, words of power. The ceremonies which attend the vesting of the priest in his hieratic robes, the rites of purification, the blessing of incense, are all paralleled in the preparations for a magical evocation. In the Latin Church the Asperges, the triple repetitions of words of power in the Kyrie, Sanctus, and Agnus, and the roll-call of angelical names with which the Preface ends, are instances of ritual acts of which the true intention would be well understood by any expert student of occultism.

In many minor observances—*i.e.*, the Rosary, with its hermetically-correct number sequences—we seem to stand on the very borderland between magician and priest. But when all this has been conceded, the religious value of these ceremonies remains unimpaired, for only under that ecstatic condition which it is the very business of Magic to induce, can the subconscious mind which is the medium of our spiritual experiences come to its own, and communicate with the transcendental world. The appeal of religion is not to the intellect but to the soul. Its theology may or may not convince the reason: only its *Magic* will open the inner door. Therefore Christianity, when she founds her external system on sacraments and symbols, on prayer and praise, and insists on the power of the pure and self-denying will and the "magic chain" of congregational worship, joins hands with those Magi whose gold, frankincense, and myrrh were the first gifts that she received.

This was the truth which Eliphas Lévi reached. When he began his investigations of Magic he was in no sense a mystic. The illumination which he offers in his earliest work is upon the intellectual, never upon the spiritual, plane. As he progressed the Universal Medicine worked in him, and he read deeper and deeper into the esoteric and spiritual meanings of the doctrines of hermetic science. Hence his willingness, at last, to avail himself of the active magic of the Church. Biographers have assailed him for the "inconsistency" of this reconciliation, and for his tendency to explain away or modify in later works positions rather arrogantly assumed in his early writings. But it is just this childlike exhibition of his own mental and spiritual processes which constitutes the value of Eliphas Lévi's books, both to the psychologist and to younger adventurers who are bound on his own quest.

That quest, as no student of mysticism needs to be reminded, is always one. In Hermetic language, its end may be deduced by analogy, apprehended by faith, achieved by obedience to the four laws of initiation: *Oser, Vouloir, Savoir, Se Taire*. It is the quest on which the true adepts of Magic have always been set, though disguising their standards with many strange devices and mystifications because of the enemies upon the road. It is their glory that they have been able, of all the pilgrims on that way, to proclaim the unique dogma of the true Catholicity, which for Eliphas Lévi, the last of their great initiates, proved the word of power which reconciled reason with faith:— "*Je crois qu'un même espoir vit sous tous les symboles.*"

This is the defence of Magic.

* * *

Outro: Ecstatic Connection

This essay is often thought of as a youthful anomaly or indiscretion instead of as being part of the spiritual juggernaut she becomes with the publication of *Mysticism* (1911). Perhaps, though, this text gives an essential insight into the connection that she made between her desire to understand the ecstasy she felt with the unseen world and a more orthodox Christianity she would embrace in the years to come.

In the second part of her essay, Underhill describes both the importance and the degradation of the phrase "Astral Light." But then how is one to describe in words the ineffable force that drives the universe? She questions whether such a phrase should be tossed out because of its misuse by those who would simply become stage magicians, those who would use the great power of the universe to perform conjuring tricks. She describes how ritual and its complicated accoutrement are meant to bewilder the senses to shut out the seen world so as to better perceive the world that lies beyond the veil. The reason magic is so looked down upon is that others would use it to take money from the gullible. It is clear in her defense of Lévi and of Magic that she is also clarifying her own connection to the ineffable that began her quest for meaning, which would, like in the case of Lévi, lead her back to Christianity.

To understand the depth of her mystical Christian belief, a belief that would lead to her huge output in print and her eventual status as a revered person in the Anglican Church, this essay stands as a signpost marking an end of an important era in her life. The intellectual curiosity that her biographer Christopher J.R. Armstrong describes as the beginning point has one major precursor that her short fiction and poetry explores: an encounter with that unseen world and the struggle to express in writing the boundaries of that experience. Underhill's creative output during the years leading up to the publication of "A Defence of Magic" must stand as foundational to her life's work.

ACKNOWLEDGMENTS

We traveled far and wide to research and write this book, and we have many people to thank for making it possible. We spent days in the British Library and are grateful to the staff there—and to librarians everywhere—for their dedication to preserving the records of human civilization. We'd like especially to thank Mr. Richard Wilkinson for his kind permission to use "At The End of the Garden." Thank you to Dr. David Sherwood, Director of the Frances Donaldson Library at Nashotah House. We also want to thank Oliver Snaith at King's College London for his generous assistance in opening the Evelyn Underhill archive to us. The archivists at Yale University's Library were helpful in making *Horlick's Magazine* available to us. Thank you to Christopher Pote, Archivist at the Virginia Theological Seminary for helping us to find the *Horlick's Magazine* stories. Bill would like to recognize the support of the Faculty Development Program at the University of Wisconsin Oshkosh. Finally, we'd like to thank the librarians at the University of Wisconsin Oshkosh—Matthew Reinhardt,

Kelly Johnson, Ane Carriveau, and Lynette Kopetsky—for helping us to track down many of the materials we consulted for this project.

WORKS CITED

Armstrong, Christopher J. R. *Evelyn Underhill (1875-1941): An Introduction to Her Life and Writings*. A. R. Mowbray & Co., 1975, London.

Bridgers, Lynn. "The Head and the Heart: William James and Evelyn Underhill on Mysticism." *William James Studies*, vol. 9, 2012, 27–36. *EBSCOhost*, search.ebscohost.com/login.aspx?direct=true&AuthType=ip,uid&db=mzh&AN=2019100946&site=ehost-live&scope=site.

Christopher, Joe R. "The Making of a Mystic." Review of *The Making of a Mystic: New and Selected Letters of Evelyn Underhill*, edited by Carol Poston. *Mythlore* vol. 30, no. 1/2, 163-168. https://www.mythsoc.org/reviews/the-making-of-a-mystic.htm

Cropper, Margaret. *Life of Evelyn Underhill*. Harper and Brothers, 1958.

Eriugena, John Scotus. *Periphyseon (The Division of Nature)*, translated by I. P. Sheldon-Williams, revised by John J. O'Meara, Dumbarton Oaks, 1987.

"For Lassies and Laddies." *Hearth and Home*, vol. I, no. 24, 29 Oct. 1891, 530. Nineteenth Century UK Periodicals, New York Public Library.

Gillard, William, James Reitter, and Robert Stauffer, editors. *The Spark of Modernism: Twenty Speculative Stories and*

Writings That Defined an Era, 1886-1939. McFarland Press, 2023.

Greene, Dana. *Evelyn Underhill: Artist of the Infinite Life.* Crossroad, 1990.

Horlick's Magazine and Home Journal for Australia, India and the Colonies Vol. I, II, and III., James Elliott & Co., 1904-1905.

Holy Rule of St. Benedict, The. Translated by Rev. Boniface Verheyen, OSB, https://ccel.org/ccel/benedict/rule/rule.i.html. Accessed 22 Nov. 2022.

Jantzen, Grace. "Legacy of Evelyn Underhill." *Feminist Theology*, vol. 2, no 4, 1993, 79-100.

Julian of Norwich. "Revelations of Divine Love." *Revelations Of Divine Love*, https://www.gutenberg.org/files/52958/52958-h/52958-h.htm.

Lévi, Eliphas. *The History of Magic*, translated by Arthur Edward Waite, William Rider & Son, Limited, 1922.

---. *Transcendental Magic, Its Doctrine and Ritual*, translated by Arthur Edward Waite, Rider and Company, 1958.

Lovecraft, Howard Phillip. "Pickman's Model." *The Complete Fiction*, edited by S.T. Joshi, Barnes & Noble, 2011, 380-390.

---. "Supernatural Horror in Literature." *The Complete Fiction*, edited by S.T. Joshi, Barnes & Noble, 2011, 1041-1098.

MacDonald, George. *Phantastes.* Schocken Books, 1982.

Machen, Arthur. "The Great God Pan." *Collected Fiction, Volume 1*, edited by S.T. Joshi, Hippocampus Press, 2019, 217-268.

---. *Mist and Mystery*, edited by Christopher Tompkins, Darkly Bright Press, 2022.

Milbank, Alison. "Holy Terrors: The Mystical Gothic of Arthur Machen, Evelyn Underhill, and Charles

Williams. *God and the Gothic: Religion, Romance, and Reality in the English Literary Tradition*, Oxford University Press, 2018.

Pius X. *Pascendi Dominici Gregis.* Libreria Editrice Vaticana. http://www.vatican.va/content/pius-x/en/encyclicals/documents/hf_p-x_enc_19070908_pascendi-dominici-gregis.html, 1907.

Porete, Marguerite. *The Mirror of Simple Souls*, edited by Clare Kirchberger, Benziger Brothers, 1927.

Ramsey, Michael. "Evelyn Underhill." *Religious Studies,* vol. 12, no. 3, 1976, pp. 273-279.

Staudt, Kathleen Henderson. "Rereading Evelyn Underhill's Mysticism." *Spiritus*, vol. 12, no. 1, 2012, 113–28.

Sweetser, Wesley D. *Arthur Machen.* Twayne, 1964.

Underhill, Sir Arthur. *Change and Decay: The Recollections and Reflections of an Octagenarian Bencher.* Butterworth & Company (Publishers) Ltd., 1938.

Underhill, Evelyn. "At the End of the Garden." Unpublished manuscript, 35 pages. King's College London Library Archives, Collection K/PP75.

---. *A Bar-Lamb's Ballad Book.* Kegan Paul, Trench Trübner & Co. Ltd., 1902.

---. *The Collected Papers of Evelyn Underhill*, edited by Lucy Menzies, Longman's, Green, and Co., 1946.

---. *The Column of Dust.* Methuen, 1909.

---. "The Death of a Saint." *Horlick's Magazine and Home Journal for Australia, India and the Colonies Vol. II.,* James Elliott & Co., 1904-1905, 173-177.

---. "Defence of Magic, A." *Putnam's Monthly*, vol. III, October 1907 - March 1908, 177-185. https://archive.org/details/underhill-1907-magic/mode/2up?view=theater

---. *Essentials of Mysticism.* E. P. Dutton & Co., 1920.

---. "A Green Mass." *Horlick's Magazine and Home Journal for Australia, India and the Colonies Vol. II.* James Elliott & Co., 1904-1905, 445-448.

---. *Grey World, The.* Scriptoria Books, 2014.

---. *Immanence: A Book of Verses.* J. M. Dent & Sons, Ltd., 1913.

---. "The Ivory Tower." *Horlick's Magazine and Home Journal for Australia, India and the Colonies Vol. III.,* James Elliott & Co., 1904-1905, 207-211.

---. *Letters of Evelyn Underhill, The.* Edited by Charles Williams. Longmans, Green and Company, 1944.

---. *Lost Word: A Spiritual Journey, The.* William Heinemann, 1907.

---. *Making of a Mystic, The: New and Selected Letters of Evelyn Underhill*, edited by Carol Poston, University of Illinois Press, 2010.

---. *Miracles of Our Lady St. Mary, The.* E. P. Dutton & Co., 1906.

---. *Modern Guide to the Ancient Quest for the Holy*, edited by Dana Greene, State University of New York Press, 1988.

---. "The Mountain Image." *Horlick's Magazine and Home Journal for Australia, India and the Colonies Vol. II.* James Elliott & Co., 1904-1905, 375-380.

---. *Mystic Way, The. J. M. Dent and Sons, 1913.*

---. *Mysticism: The Preeminent Study in the Nature and Development of Spiritual Consciousness. Image Books, 1990.*

---. *"Our Lady of the Gate." Horlick's Magazine and Home Journal for Australia, India and the Colonies Vol. II.* James Elliott & Co., 1904-1905, 243-247.

---. *Practical Mysticism.* E. P. Dutton & Co., 1914.

---. *Shrines and Cities of France and Italy. Longman, Green & Co., 1949.*

---. *Theophanies: A Book of Verses. J. M. Dent & Sons Limited, 1916.*

---. *"Threefold Quest, The." The Treasury Illustrated Magazine*, vol. VIII, no. 52, January 1907, 341-347.

Waite, Arthur Edward. "A Grey World." *Collected Poems of Arthur Edward Waite in Two Volumes*. William Rider & Son, Limited, 1906, 45-47.

---. "Of the Morality of the Lost Word." *A Book of Mystery and Vision.* Philip Wellby, 1902, 67-125.

---. *Shadows of Life and Thought: A Retrospective Review in the Form of Memoirs.* Selwyn and Blount, Paternoster House, 1937.

Whitlark, James. "Evelyn Underhill (6 December 1875-15 June 1941)." *Late Nineteenth-and Early Twentieth-Century British Women Poets*, edited by William B. Thesing, vol. 240, Gale, 2001, 283-292.

Williams, Charles. *The Letters of Evelyn Underhill.* Longmans, Green & Co., 1943.

Wrigley-Carr, R. "Darkness and Light in Evelyn Underhill." *Journal of Spiritual Formation and Soul Care*, vol. 12, no. 1, 2019, 135-151.

www.ingramcontent.com/pod-product-compliance
Lightning Source LLC
Jackson TN
JSHW021059060825
88529JS00001B/1